PETER
OWEN

A PETER OW

WEN

CW00346692

design illustration Thomi Wroblewski

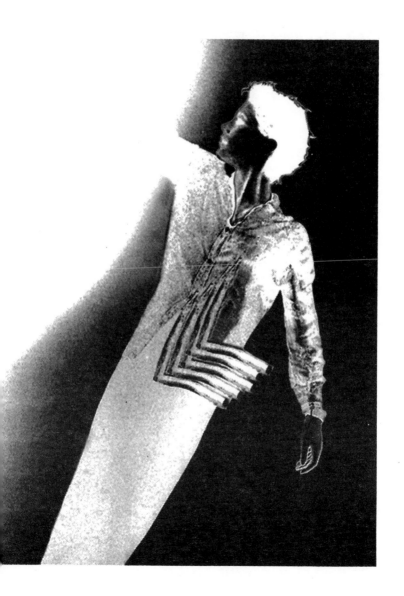

 *Chasing Black Rainbows*

By the same author
(published by Peter Owen)

Fiction
Inhabiting Shadows
Isidore (Lautréamont)
When the Whip Comes Down (Marquis de Sade)
Diamond Nebula

Non-Fiction
Madness – The Price of Poetry
Lipstick, Sex and Poetry (autobiography)
Delirium: An Interpretation of Rimbaud

Poetry
Black Sugar: Trisexual Poems

Jeremy Reed

Chasing Black Rainbows

A novel about Antonin Artaud

PETER OWEN *London & Chester Springs PA*

PETER OWEN PUBLISHERS
73 Kenway Road London SW5 0RE

Peter Owen books are distributed in the USA by
Dufour Editions Inc. Chester Springs PA 19425–0449

First published in Great Britain 1994
© Jeremy Reed 1994

All Rights Reserved.
No part of this publication may be reproduced in
any form or by any means without the written
permission of the publishers.

ISBN 0–7206–0924–0

A catalogue record for this book is available from
the British Library

Printed and made in Great Britain by Biddles of Guildford

For Fanchon Fröhlich

We all have dispersed consciousness through all our body parts, wandering wombs; we are all hysterics. Authenticity is in the illusion, playing it, seeing through it from within as we play it, like an actor sees through his mask and can only see in this way.

James Hillman, *Healing Fictions*

Preface

A revolutionary theorist of the stage and producer of avant-garde drama, a poet and an actor, Antonin Artaud (1896–1948) is more than any of these things an individual committed to advancing art to extremes of expression. Artaud's life and work are about pushing vision to the edge and beyond it, an act of creative subversion that places the poet in the true role of anarchic visionary.

My novel is centred on Artaud's madness, the pathologically diagnosed schizophrenia which was the cause of his undergoing nine years' incarceration in mental hospitals, most notably at Rodez, where Artaud came under the care of Dr Gaston Ferdière, one of the pioneers of the innovative electroshock therapy.

My Artaud is of course a fictional one, and some of the people who touched on his life, like Anaïs Nin and June and Henry Miller, are worked into the novel as characters realized independent of his consciousness. Nin's *Incest* is one of the sources for her polysexual propensities both in her life and in the context of my fiction.

But principally my theme is one I have explored in my own life and through the personae I have adopted in two previous novels, *Isidore* and *When the Whip Comes Down*, which is belief in the poet as one who changes the universe and risks everything by this undertaking. It is not a romantic ideal that the poet sacrifices his life to madness, it is often a truth. Artaud savaged the status quo through the powers of his imagination, and this novel looks towards the creation of a world in which imagination becomes reality. Where else is there to go?

Jeremy Reed

 *Chasing Black Rainbows*

Chapter 1

Even before birth, I remember a dream, a pre-natal revelation of myself as the chosen one. I was in a wheelbarrow being pushed through heavy traffic, the unlikely vehicle negotiating a spiral course between cars pulled up at the lights, and I was one of two heads attached to the body being conveyed on that hazardous journey. We were a boy and a girl contending for the sexless torso. I can remember the big red light freezing the impatient drivers. Someone had a passenger-seat window rolled down, and without warning a blunt-headed snake poked through the gap and hit the little girl's jugular. She died immediately, the venom injected into her bloodstream.

That was my beginning. I recollected the dream content much later, but it happened. At Rodez, the doctors attributed my inner reality to hallucinatory psychosis, and to a schizophrenic doubling of the personality. I spat. And the snake returned. It uncoiled at my feet, gold lozenges diamonding into its black scales. I had christened my dead sister Anne-Marie. The snake was her accusatory form of reincarnation. I knew that if I split it open, she would be there. The size of a doll, she would make hissing noises in the corner. And at night she would sit on my nether lip and sing me to sleep.

And there was another form of beginning: 4 September 1896, at 15 rue du Jardin des Plantes, near the Marseille zoo. An event in which I was an involuntary participant. So much must have happened at that moment of birth about which I recollect nothing. It's as though we're no one for a long time, just the idea of a person, and later on someone comes to inhabit that mind. It could be anyone stepped in from the street. Eventually I, Antonin Artaud, elected to assume an identity. I became. And then I deconstructed each of the personae I adopted.

I begin with fragments. When I came to Rodez in January 1943, the asylum in the south-west of France, whose head psychiatrist was Gaston Ferdière, I had in my mind buried Antonin Artaud. Years of starvation, mistreatment and persecution at the asylum of Ville-Évrard had given me a body thin as a coil of rope discarded on a bed. I had officiated at my own burial. Artaud was committed to the earth in a red velvet cloak sewn with pearls. Under the middle one of three yew trees grouped behind the ruins of Sade's château at La Coste, his imperishable body was kept on recall. Incorruptible, immutable, it would wait to be repossessed. The new identity I had chosen was that of Antonin Nalpas. And when Nalpas died, he would be preserved by cryonics, burial in ice, which would have him conserved like a big fish at consistent temperature. Artaud was too brutalized to live. Humiliated, impoverished, his work seen as the gestural imprecations of a psychotic, he had been prodded like an animal rounded up for the slaughterhouse; his ravings were the breath-modulated self-defence of a man hunted by doctors, nurses, the police. I had at that time to let him go. He was a burnt-out emissary on the road to a drug-sustained vision.

Mostly they leave me alone. I hum and make violent gestures towards the hallucinated figures who gain access to my room, my mind. One of them floats on my breath. Others break through, and threaten by their facility to earth themselves in my head.

14

There's one who comes leading a blind white horse, red sores on its flanks. The man wants something; he would like to confiscate my words and feed them to the injured horse. And on better days there's no one there. Only Ferdière and his staff policing the corridors. The violent shrieks of inmates, the rhythmic vibration of my breath tunnelling through the metal door.

And what is it that brings me to this state, asks of me that my inner disposition should be so radically unattuned to the status quo? To whom is it accountable that at this moment someone is forcing their fist through a window, another celebrating orgasmic intensity, and still another meditating on white light? And why am I, Antonin Nalpas, sitting here the victim of electroshock therapy, while jackals brush against my desk, my legs, recalling how as a youth I received a knife wound in front of the Église des Réformés in Marseille, a pimp's blade which marked me for life, brandished me an outlaw? Did it all begin then? The breath forced out of my body, the man's black eyes implanting the curse which has leaked through my emaciated body, his leather jacket wrinkled along the sleeves, two gold rings bunched on his knuckles. He was sudden. His brute flesh in contact with mine. There was a young girl on the other side of the street, pushing her skirt up provocatively to a black stocking top, an equally black suspender strap. It was like theatre. It wasn't that I was interested in sexual acquisition. I was curious, in the way that one often doesn't know why. Looking happens involuntarily. The girl had taken my eye all the way to her black panties, and the man jumped me. He slashed me on the right, between the lower ribs, the incision only a surface one, but the confrontational shock of metal opening out my blood to view left me huddled within myself, as I made my way back home through alleys, a wolf not wishing to be seen by daylight, a pariah searching for the edge of the desert to begin a long, stony exile.

There wasn't a way back to my room. The mental space that had opened up confounded me with a new complex geography of the unconscious. The houses in the neighbourhood had changed.

They were suddenly windowless, asymmetrical, displaced. A sailor was having a girl up against a wall, lifting her on to his pivot, her silk stockings knotted in a dress bow round his back. He didn't modulate his rhythm when he heard my footsteps, but I was a somnambulist, I walked as a projection of myself, someone seeing himself on cinema, disconnected, on the edge of dematerializing for ever.

My father was absent on one of his endless trading journeys, and my mother, a Levantine Greek, was out on my return to the house. I can still see my relief, hear the relaxation in my breathing, when I realized the house was empty. I checked the kitchen floor to be sure I wasn't leaving a trail of blood spots. She must have taken my brother and sister with her and gone out for a baguette. There was a smell of cooking. Couscous. And she had slipped her house sandals for the white high heels she wore to go out in the local neighbourhood, with its cafés, urinous scents, cosmopolitan bustle, its hookers with red oval mouths and constrictively tight skirts. There was a blind man who hung out on the corner, squeezing a harmonica, a series of notes which became inseparable in my mind from dusk, contemplation, the blue ring I wore without my mother ever seeing it. The ring was my secret. I kept it concealed in a hiding-place in my drawer; the one I guarded with territorial hostility from my brother and sister.

I made my way to my room, knowing that I would never be the same again, that something had irreparably damaged me. I took off my blood-stained shirt and examined the wound. It had formed a hexagram, an eight-pointed star. The jagged incision was entirely transformed into this compact, distinguishing symbol. I knew then that it was a sign. I had undergone a blood initiation, a ritual killing by which the child was separated from its paternity and elected by occult powers to be the chosen one. I was dazed, dissociated, sitting there with a slew of books on the bed, the precocious reading I was discouraged from pursuing at home and at school: Baudelaire, Rimbaud, Poe, a few novels published by the *NRF*. Books I had either stolen or

16

acquired through the tiny payment I received for occasional café work.

I feared being sent away again. My parents, unable to cope with the violent oscillation of my moods, the swing between mania and abject moroseness, had taken to sending me on rest-cures, periods of relaxed internment in sanatoriums. These interludes gave me the time in which to read, draw, reflect on the images that mobbed my head, their invading pressure threatening to drive me out of consciousness. I had the notion I would lose identity and become one of those transmigrational spirits who lacking bodily ties slink out of drains at noon, run with the wolf in the hills, cling to the belly of a horse as it stampedes over a cliff edge. My voice would be heard declaiming on a deserted building site, violent at nightfall, pitched at a low tone in the student's attic, a whisper in the rat's mouth as it runs through the autumn leaves.

My wound was the affirmation of my identity. I convinced myself that the pimp had dematerialized and that he was appointed by an order to find me. And the girl? She probably had her legs round a sailor now, her bottom rocking a creaky bed, her payment slipped into a stocking-top. I listened to my thoughts in the same way as I am doing this moment at Rodez. There's an audible momentum to thought, a hiss to the inner stream of consciousness that's discernible like the static interference on a tape. I learnt to hear the modulations of sound expressed by my inner dialogue. I sustained meditation in the gaps between images, prolonged pauses in which I would attempt to erase the blurs left by the disturbing punctums on which I focused. I was already experimenting with my mind; the body would follow later. I made of myself a psychophysical laboratory. My innate masochism demanded I become my work. The pain involved in writing was worked out in my diaphragm, my abdomen, my bowels. Mental inspiration demanded a correspondingly painful physical extraction. When a poem was in the making, its black heart jumped like a toad across the page. Writing became the restructuring of my neurology; a drum-beat that alerted my nerve endings to the vibrational rhythm of experience. I still shriek when I work, and lack of opium and heroin inside exacerbates my condition.

When I first took opium, a substance prescribed for me by Dr Dardel during my summer visit to the sanatorium at Neuchâtel, I experienced a profound sense of having discovered the reality which had always eluded me. For once I was relieved of the sense of being an open wound. The poppy eliminated all traces of temporal anguish. In my mind I was dreaming in a rocking-chair at a disused railway station. Sitting opposite me was a woman, who had caught the curve of the rainbow in her mouth. Descending out of the sky, supported by that coloured arc, an open-carriaged train was making an indefinite journey towards her. The goods carriages were stashed with white crosses, coffins, and a black snake was basking on one of the disorderly heaps. I was filled with the presentiment that someone or something was coming to meet me. My only fear was that the woman wouldn't be able to sustain the weight of the rainbow. I was expecting it to snap, the train to become derailed and somersault out of the sky. But it didn't. It neither advanced nor receded, but at some stage of my reverie, from which time was absent, a white cross began its own independent journey towards me. And what I saw on this cross was my name, Antonin Artaud, and the date of my death, 4 March 1948.

The numerals burnt into my consciousness. They became an obsession, one of the many that continue to terrorize me. Each time I take opium, I attempt to rediscover the vision. I want to erase the conception that my death is prefigured by malign occult forces. I want to eradicate the notion that I shall ever die. I am like the Tarahumara Indians in Mexico, some of whom live to be eight hundred.

But opium is a habit that I'm supposed to be without at Rodez. Ferdière claims that my mania is increased by the experimental drugs I use as another extension to vision. I want to deny every other reality but the imagination.

Bits of my life break free of the wound I have become. The hexagram remains indelibly tattooed on my body; but to doctors it is invisible. My mother never saw it when she came back from shopping. She attributed my state of shock to panic. She had grown used to my fluctuating moods, the dark ones that sat on me like a mountain, the elevated ones that had me run outside into the street proclaiming my genius.

But there was a woman who traced the outline of my star with her finger. Anaïs Nin. She broke into my absolute moral solitude. I was inside, hiding from her, but she walked into me, broke through the transparent glass, and although I resisted it, she knew parts of me, assessed my pivotal centre, undid me, her fingers coaxing me erect, three red fingernails running my length, making of it a hypersensitive drum-skin. At La Coupole we kissed, the heat darting along her tongue and injecting me with flame. Her silk dress sat on her body like the shiver of wind on a lake, a black sinuous mould precariously suspended by spaghetti straps. This woman's sensitivity was such that she had only to breathe on a man and he would come. Her voice, her intimate laughter fanned tropical storms in the blood. At that time I wasn't celibate, intent on conserving my spermatozoa for fear of its occult appropriation, but erotically taut, looking to find an esoteric marriage through the body.

But this woman tormented me. She was always with someone else somewhere else. And when she wasn't making love with her eyes, her toes, her fingers, she withdrew into a private world of dream. She disappeared in order to write, to establish a geography of the psyche, an intimate re-creation of the heightened moments that comprised her life. She cooked my heart in black juices. Presented it to me on a plate at Louveciennes. I wanted her and I didn't. I was Heliogabalus, the mad Roman emperor. I saluted the crowds from our taxi on the way to the Gare Saint-Lazare. The compressed rage in my Reichstag voice had people look back at the car. The driver stopped and wanted to throw me out, but Anaïs crossed her black silk stockinged legs, and we continued on our way. She told the driver I was drunk and that I wouldn't cause trouble. She let her skirt ride up marginally, unconsciously, but the hand I placed on her knee was rejected.

19

When I got down and knelt, she stared straight ahead as though she had eliminated me from her life. She was looking out at a Paris from which I was absent. Her red shoes were different in close-up, smaller, wrinkled round the pointed toes, objects that seemed to have stepped out of a painting and fitted themselves to her stockinged feet.

The driver must have thought my head was intending to disappear up her skirt, for he brought the car to an abrupt halt and shouted at us to get out. We stood on the pavement next to a vagrant with a parrot sitting on his shoulder. Anaïs showed no visible signs of displeasure. She suggested we go back to my room. My small attic on the Left Bank contained nothing but a bed, a desk, a chair. My only possessions were my manuscripts, my photographs, my opium pipe, the stash I kept in a sachet under my pillow.

She sat on the chair, her legs made weightless by the transparency of black silk, her eye observing every small detail, as though she had the ability to apprehend the unspoken thought as well as the one crystallized by speech. She was taking in my shadow life, the double who sits on the inside, confident he will never be found out in the dual dialogue he is conducting in silence. And it was the inner person Anaïs wanted to know. The physical me, Antonin Artaud, was of less interest to her. His mania, and contraction into silence, his terrifying and obsessive declarations of love had her retreat, back off as though she was watching a tiger stalk her in a dream. She was opposite me but further away than a near planet. At some point I got up and told her that our relationship would end in murder. We each desired something that the other couldn't give. I wanted her unconditional love, her extreme sensuality, and she wanted me to reverse roles, bring the other me to the exterior so she could live fascinated by that creature of metaphysical anguish. To her, I was valuable only as a fire-walker running along a line of red coals at the edge of a precipice. The human me was disposable. My flesh, my blood, my bones, the organism within which my work was contained, were found lacking, despite her praise of

20

my eyes, my face, the inimitable suffering written into my features. And when a woman or a man finds one physically attractive, and yet rejects the idea of sex, the internal scar never really heals. At least mine didn't. It was my obsessional quest for the irretrievable that fascinated her. She thought my madness was a slow-leaking poison, that the venom would be transferred to her veins by way of a physical relationship.

We left my room and walked along the Seine, stopping here and there to riffle through book-trays. The wind mapped out a spine on the river's back. There was a young man with his arm round a girl's waist, his hand shifting from her broad red leather belt to her bottom. Her laugh indicated her pleasure at his advances. My separation from the intimacy of their experience, the girl's chiffon scarf lifting as they walked, was one of existential terror. I realized I could never be that, never know such casual abandon. My hands were blocked in ice. And even if my compulsion was to do the same to Anaïs, caress her intimately through her tight silk dress, then my gestures were frozen. There would have been a division between my mind and body, I would have been self-conscious that my hand was outlining an erotic calligraphy on her bottom. My mind would have been somewhere else, measuring the ravine in which Poe was locked inside a golden cage, fingers tearing at the bars, a lion looking in from the outside.

I remember the occasion, for as we walked along, so the books and manuscripts I was carrying fell to the ground. Suddenly anonymous, depersonalized, pages scattered on the gust, went off on an origami trail, equally scattering my thoughts as I went in pursuit of bits of my mind. Head down, on all fours, my fingers stabbed at the elusive sheets. But what I was seeing on the cold paving stones was hexagrams, pentagrams, marked out in blood. Livid, red, cabbalistic signs had been placed there as a conspiratorial plot. I froze, unable to move, reminded of the blue-suited pimp who had slashed me in Marseille, aware too that Anaïs was wearing scarlet shoes, and that there was an association between those and the constellated hex that had been placed on me. And the magic symbols were closing in an autonomous circle round me. I expected them to jump and brand my skin, so that my face, my neck, the backs of my hands would be patterned with red stars. I would be a surrealist exhibit, the living embodiment of Breton's desire to transform reality into the marvellous. And at the same time I was convinced that if I jumped into the river, I would be clean.

I must have lifted myself up to the parapet, and hands were drawing me back, restraining the wired tension in my solar plexus, pulling me with the same insistence as the river would have asserted in dragging me under. I was brought back, and Anaïs was standing in the crowd, hands on her hips, as though she was posing for a photograph, looking at me analytically, dispassionately, dissecting the emotions that had driven me to this extreme action. I was left there, shivering, odd, a black-suited bird that had just landed from the sky. No one knew what to do with me. Someone suggested a doctor, the police, but Anaïs took charge of the situation, linked her arm through mine and guided me away from the staring crowd. They followed us as if we were two figures walking away in a film, their eyes sitting on our backs as the credits arrive on the screen and the accompanying music phases out the last narrated steps.

We continued to walk towards an imaginary future, Anaïs' arm never slackening in its grip, neither of us talking, the understanding too serious for words, the journey one of reacquainting me with life. I was like a child being led away from the scene of an accident. I didn't see the booksellers on the quays, the plane trees heavy with the glitter of wind, the anonymity of the many crossing their city. Anaïs called my attempted suicide an initiation into death. I had undergone the intentions without sublimating the action. What I recalled was the compulsion, a need that blanked out rationality, a shadow that dropped on me like a dramatic eclipse. The gravitation to die was stronger than the impulse to live.

We went and sat down in a café. I remember planting my eyes on an advertisement for Heineken and leaving them there, as though the enlarged capitals afforded the stability of a branch. The incidental could have been anything, and once I'd discovered it, I grew fixated. I heard Anaïs, but I didn't see her. Even her familiar gesture of allowing just too much of her legs to show, was something I guessed rather than observed. She wore a red, lozenge-shaped jewel at her throat, a reflection from which angled its way into my vision. I had the overpowering feeling that she was trying to break into my mind. So I had to protect my thoughts, keep them safe, the way rare goldfish are transported in damp pads of cotton wool. If she could, she would have extracted images from my head and watched them flap, fin and tail, in her cupped hands.

I was disconnected but at the same time terrified she would leave. I imagined her in other men's beds. Her acrobatic elasticity, compliancy of position, her black stockings bunched on her hands in order to heighten the sensuality of her intimate caresses. I imagined her with as many legs as a spider, her voice climbing the scale of pleasure notes, her lovers arriving by taxi, punctually every three hours. My mind invented her inventory of erotic desires. I was imagining a man removing her black chiffon panties with his lips, a red jewel coming alive at her waist, her body undulating like a belly-dancer's. Denied her body, I fumed with acute sexual jealousy. I was certain that she was making an assignation with the waiter. Off duty, he would take the train to Louveciennes. She would be expecting him. She would lead him upstairs, stepping out of her dress on the way. He would be too urgent, and her body would restrain him, lead him step by step towards ultimate pleasure.

I brooded. There wasn't anywhere for me to go, and Anaïs knew it. I was on the edge of an abyss. My internal landscape was in flames. I placed my hands face down on the table-top as the fire roared in my head. Everything was catching – the mirrors, waiters, Anaïs. I was watching an apocalyptic holocaust. I closed my eyes and there was fire inside. I opened them and I was sitting in the middle of a conflagration. Anaïs was smiling encouragingly at me. Her lipstick was the colour of cassis, her mouth articulated like an erotic bruise. She gave everyone the illusion of exclusive love. But my sense of being special didn't easily lend itself to her professed sensuality. Antonin Artaud demanded her total attention. After all, there wasn't much time. Eagles would come to walk along the river bank, lions and tigers would terrorize the streets, and I would be seen leading a file of the chosen ones towards a craft waiting at the jetty. Anaïs would grow frantic in the hysterical crowds. She would shout my name across the river, but I would be too changed to recollect that I once knew this woman.

In my mind, I was planning revenge on the world. I wanted to see the whole social structure with its conflicting ideologies destroyed. The bureaucrat motoring home would find himself confronted by collapsing buildings, craters in the road, monsters sitting on cupolas. Only those who lived through the imagination would follow me towards the rainbow I had first seen as an opium vision, and climb it into the sky. And there we would wait to reclaim the ravaged earth. I would lead a procession back through the boulevards, high grasses bushing the roads, cafés and shops overrun by globe thistles, dandelions, cow-parsley, insidious ivy spreading round table and chair. In my own blood I would write the story of the new creation, the myths, the cultural transformations, and tell of the exotic blue eagles that had come from a secret mountain retreat to make their home on the rooftops of Montmartre.

I was seeing all that within the speed and space of thought. Images forming and colliding, fictions in which I was the avenging protagonist. Anaïs was thousands of years away, self-consciously touching up her dark lipstick in a compact mirror, trying to find some route of access to my visible estrangement. But even in her discomfort she was concerned with her appearance, the arrangement of her legs, the angle at which a ring was presented to the light. She sat facing her own image and the idea of herself showed in her green eyes. Or were they violet? She was disarmed, and I protracted her suffering, forced her to feel guilt over her refusal to give me priority in her life. I wanted her to

24

consider her life, her rampant promiscuity, her refusal to equate emotions with anything but pleasure. I left her to connect with the images that represented our past. The mad, the serene, the declamatory, the passionate, they were all crowding inside her head. She was confronting our private film, viewing a different one from me, slower or faster, but involved with the same conflicts. She sipped nervously at her coffee and toyed with a bracelet. And I was enjoying the ability to inflict pain. I wanted her to break down and confess that she had humiliated me, and that in future she would devote her life to me.

But there was only a sustained silence, Anaïs adjusting a shoulder strap, checking the consistency of surface on a lacquered nail. Her adeptness with small feminine things was yet another means of concentrating on herself, a ritual that afforded inner and outer dimensions a unity.

I wanted to perform an act of violence, but I restrained myself. I kept on returning to the red capitals HEINEKEN. An ad logo was pulsating across my image of burning boats stranded by the Paris quays. I should like to have torn off her dress, lacerated the silk to expose her black panties, black bra and black suspenders. I wanted to invoke the primitive, sound a drum which would have the rudimentary gods appear with a still more rapacious and concentrated existence. The people in this café, the waiters, the pedestrians out in the cloudy afternoon, had little idea of the thin partition that separated them from the other side. I was born with the facility to hallucinate reality. It is this particular faculty that has brought me to Rodez, after I was interned in a series of whitewashed, barbarically outmoded asylums.

And today I can't work. I've returned to facing Anaïs across a café table. The scene recomposes itself, gesture by gesture. Anaïs had earlier on reminded me of my talk about 'The Theatre and the Plague' at the Sorbonne. And how I had enacted my own death on-stage. My agonized shrieks, the trancelike suspension in which I let go of myself invited ridicule, until finally the audience left, slamming doors loudly, retreating from a man

25

obsessed by empathetic death rites. And the humiliation of that performance leaked into the adversity I felt for her. They were suddenly all there, bugging the café windows with their eyes, the contingent of those who had pointed at me in the street, the psychiatrists who had brutalized me, the members of the literary world who had dismissed my writings as the fragmented visions of a madman. They were out there, conspiring, letting their eyes travel over my body like insects. On their terms, they had won. They had succeeded in forcing me into an uncompromising solitude. Surrealism had been my potential hope that my isolation could be shared, and that the individuals united by a common anarchic cause would find unlimited imaginative freedom under Breton's leadership. My expulsion from the group remained as a concealed hurt, a scar that reopened each time my paranoia grew obsessive. It was there again as part of that afternoon with Anaïs. My expulsion came with a meeting at the Prophet café on 10 December 1926. Breton's political affiliation with communism disgusted me; so too his sympathies with psychoanalytic systemization. I declared that true revolution takes place within the individual's imagination: Breton wanted to extend psychic anarchy into social revolution.

As Anaïs tried to extract me from my disquieting inner stream of consciousness, events recomposed themselves. Breton's leonine despotism, his love of life, his passionate sensuality, his words travelling around the table, but finding their epicentre in me, were met by my constraint. Silent for once, a skin stitched over another skin, I wanted to shriek, but the noise reversed itself. My hostility took the form of uncommunicativeness. I had been smoking opium earlier in the day and was preoccupied by residual visions which remained like clouds, motionless in an otherwise empty sky. Faces, a cave in which someone was sitting inside a wine bottle, a frog spitting out emeralds, diamonds and rubies, these images kept recurring, travelling round on a fixed circuit. I was inward, conscious of the pettiness of Breton's authoritarianism, my vision alighting on Paul Éluard's hand, repeatedly feeling for his glass. Breton's arrogance was deflated by my removal from the situation. I had vacated my body. He was forced to address no one. I had disappeared, in the way I was lost to Anaïs.

The waiter had slipped her a note. A secret rendezvous? Her hand closed over it, attempted to conceal the thing like a stone sits in its own shadow. Her temerity was such that she would openly scheme with one man in the presence of another. I hated her for it. I saw fangs flickering between her lips. I saw her husband kneeling in a corridor of lightning, someone flogging his back with a wet towel. A car burst across the landscape, a black limo carrying hired killers. And it must have been me they had come for. Four of them, faces hidden beneath rakish brims. They were going to shoot me from four different angles – back, front and two sides. I threw myself to the floor, upsetting glasses and cups. I was convinced that shots had rung out, that my spine, my skull and both lungs were punctured by bulletholes. And that I, Antonin Artaud, was a bloody heap of clothes on the floor.

The situation was impossible. Anaïs escorted me to the street. I was feeling for invisible wounds. The real holes were inside. They were the ones that were to bring me to Rodez. We went all the way back to Louveciennes in a taxi – I thought I was dead and being driven to a cemetery, yet I could feel a hand imparting reassurance to mine, the kneading of rings against my tremulous fingers. What I needed was heroin, the heroin that would temporarily abate my mania. Only then, in the drug's initial rush, and the subsequent removal from suffering that it instates, would I be free of my persecutors. A sachet of white powder, picked up in an alley outside a hotel, represented the realization of that intermediary state for which I searched: a suspension between life and death, participating in neither, and secure in my neutral state. Heroin was my surrogate suicide, a way of detaching myself so totally from poverty and nervous depression that I became someone else. I had concealed on me sufficient traces to roll a number of DCs – the dirty cigarettes which were my habit, as opposed to intravenously mainlining the substance.

The journey to Louveciennes happened independent of me. All I remember is that the car seemed to be swallowed through a hole, and we were there, the sky lit by red streaks, the house screened by oaks and plane trees. There was a fire in the bedroom, the heavy blue curtains were drawn against the coming night. The atmosphere was one of intimacy, the air loaded with hints of the perfumes Anaïs used to make up. And in my state of paranoia, the sensuous undertones implied by my being in a woman's bedroom brought on a state of perverse asceticism. I froze. I was ice tinctured with lemon; a sorbet that wouldn't melt. I could hear the insistent reverberation of an engine somewhere, as though a car was approaching but never arrived. And then I realized it was my hands that were shaking, and that the blood was pounding in my ears. Even if I had wanted to, I couldn't have touched this woman. It was as though she paralysed my impulse. And when she excused herself to slip into a kimono and I caught sight of her body through the screen, her full breasts released from a bra, her only clothing a pair of black silk panties, I lacked response. I was too far back in my head. An occupant of apocalyptic inner space.

I sat on the edge of a chair, rather than on the bed. She was fluent, relaxed, conscious of her powers to allure. I bunched myself into the role of the untouchable one; the man whose inner thoughts were too preoccupying to risk admission of company. Anaïs was talking to me of poetry, my poetry, and of how my individuality spat from each word I wrote. To read me, she was saying, was like facing the defensive ferocity of a trapped animal. She saw me as taking the reader by the throat and demanding absolute submission. I was, she said, re-enacting the violence I had experienced from my knife wound, on the reader. My words inflicted scars in the eyes, the throat, the abdomen, the genitals. While she talked, she arranged her body with the abandon of a cat. She was convinced of the importance of my prophetic role. I was the one whose belly would be dragged over fire. Hieroglyphs would be branded on the soles of my feet. Anaïs got inside me the way one goes up

28

a dark alley in search of a whore. She looked into doorways, glanced over her shoulder to be sure she wasn't being followed, scrutinized figures waiting key in hand to take the stranger upstairs. Only she stopped short of the final room in which I sat, a lion drowsing beside my feet, the book of hallucinations in my hand.

And in advancing, she beat on every door in the corridor. She surprised lovers in their moment of ecstasy, sleepers who dreamt of burning houses, sailors masturbating on rickety beds, a man taking out his eyes and replacing them with emeralds. She ran into a labyrinth in search of me. There were monsters who reared out of shadows, a god carrying his decapitated head, soldiers starved on a mountain ledge, men being buggered in back-room bars, a lawyer declaring himself a prophet at a business conference, a pilot unable to relocate the earth, a whole metamorphic spectrum of images flickering through the various levels of my unconscious. And when I looked at Anaïs I saw her hand bloodied from repeatedly banging at doors. Her knuckles were a scarlet rose; and I, instead of relenting, went deeper into myself. I went from one impenetrable room to another, locking doors behind me, throwing away the keys. I was in flight to somewhere I had never been, the back end of the night, the reverse side of consciousness, which is madness. And I knew Anaïs would never dare look for me in those broken places, with fire cracking the stones and apes standing on rocks, pelting each other with offal. I was in retreat, risking places to which I hope never to return.

And then my voice was coming back at me. It was I who was declaiming so vehemently, directing my internal anguish at a woman, the world, the emptiness of space. I was contorting my face to a ball of crumpled paper. My tongue was the whip across a flagellant's back. And when I stopped, it was as though a judgement of the world was suspended. Anaïs was white-faced, cowering in a corner of the room, too nervous to speak coherently. What she had lived through, she would never forget; but I remembered almost nothing of my diatribe.

And today, at Rodez, furiously scribbling, or adding to the endless fragments I commit to paper, I relive the beauty and terror of my existence. My leaving the house in the early hours of the morning, storming out through the wet leaves, after Anaïs had received telephone calls which were future assignations. Unable to get into her bed that night, the waiter was arranging a date for tomorrow at midnight, his erection already growing in response to her intimate voice. The next night he would arouse her again and again, their bodies would be the dance of two twisted geometries, and he would leave at dawn, but in different circumstances.

As I broke away from the house I had the impression that the statue in the garden lifted its hand. A white marble salutation. A sign for me to continue. I hurried on, not caring how I would get back to Paris. The need to hurt Anaïs was stronger than the discomfort I would experience in the cold, thumbing for a lift at an unlucky hour, cursing everyone and everything on earth for the sense of alienation that was constantly mine.

I stood there under a blue-black sky, a slight hint of rose showing in the east and a violent shower whipping my legs, driving its liquid crystals across the road. In a few minutes I was drenched. Not a car in sight. A truck lumbered by, headlights swimming in the wall of rain, and went on without stopping. I followed the churn of its engine, its battered, saurian progress through the dark. Something about this great hulk of wounded reverberating metal hit a discordant note in my mind. It seemed to represent the cold, unresponsive nature of external things. Inventions that were removed from human appeal, the autonomous as it functioned through artificial intelligence.

After a while I started walking, oblivious of the rain, holding to the centre of the road, so cars would be forced to come to an abrupt halt. All I could hear was the torrential drumming of rain. My shoes leaked; my knuckles were stung by liquid nails. As I stood there, fuming against the system of things which had me suffer, I was acutely aware that I had nowhere to go. The bare attic I called home, had no mark of my identity on its walls. It knew me as a wolf. Hungry, alert in the night hours, someone slipping out to the streets for a nocturnal itinerary of the city and returning broken at dawn. If I never returned, simply asked for my manuscripts to be collected by a friend, I would again be no one and an inhabitant of nowhere. I felt predestined to be excluded from death as well as life. If I could have peeled the skin from my body and walked out on myself, I might have known some temporary form of respite. My voice was a torrent of obscenities. I raved against the nature of existence, contesting the commitment to death which came of being born. And the rain slammed down.

I was too fixated by my inner dialogue to hear a car approaching. The violent, squealing feedback of applied brakes, the car slewing to the right and stopping just short of a tree, had me throw myself to the ground. My hands were scuffed by grit on the road's surface, my knees torn on impact with metal. The driver had jumped out of the car and was shouting insults at me. I could have killed him, his car would have been a write-off, only a madman walks dead centre down the middle of a road. Only a madman.

'Fuck you,' he shrieked.

When I got back to Paris by way of a truck carrying farm produce, the driver making me sit in the back under a tarpaulin, I was shaking with cold and fever. The sky was carnation red over Les Halles. There was a shark inside my head, grinning for battle.

But I was plotting. I lay low for five days, not eating, just sitting up to smoke opium or dull myself with heroin. My sexual fantasies of men with Anaïs were incandescent. She accommodated their every wish. I wanted to ease into her back passage and know the dark cave at the centre of the world. I would work in a solitude independent of those who aspired to literary fame. I was giving birth to the creation who has ended up as the victim of psychiatric barbarity.

And I waited. Waited for the world to come to my attic. I expected its immensity to knock on my door, the messenger carrying the Pacific Ocean in one hand, the Atlantic in the other. The Mediterranean would be in his right eye, the Adriatic in his left. But no one came. I grew progressively colder and hungrier. I could feel my skin narrow on my bones. I was kept alive by residual traces of drugs. I should like to have placed my own body in the opium pipe and watched it burn.

After a week I got out from under the blankets and sat by the window. I cursed Anaïs for her promiscuity. I saw the hanging man in the sky, the tarot symbol visible above Paris, while aircraft dipped into glideways before landing. The high-rise blocks were brutally mirrored by the evening sun. I sat waiting for the messenger. An angel or a cop. A pimp or a drag queen. Someone or no one. The pedestrians in the street were supernumeraries. They could have belonged to any time any place. The lost ones, unquestioningly finding a way through the city's arterial maze. In my mind I let my hands drop to the pavement below, and like startled creatures they ran away into hiding. One ran into a café and perched on a woman's knee, the other sat outside a bookshop, waiting for the truth to arrive.

The night came and I waited. And now it's a nurse entering my room who intrudes on my writing. I am wanted somewhere else. Ferdière will scrutinize my progress. The mad are constantly answerable to their inferiors. My thoughts have always to be corrected, their direction twisted to a tangent. It's a game, my sentences are flies that settle in his mouth, before he spits them out in an altered context. Ferdière represents evil. If he unbuttoned his shirt, his stomach would ripple with black scales. And I am made to feel grateful that they keep me here, assisted by welfare, while I slowly starve.

One day I shall strangle him, and that will be the end of it. Millions of coloured birds will appear in the sky over Rodez. The mad will run into the four corners of the earth and proclaim a new civilization. But for the moment I follow the nurse acquiescently. Anaïs is a long way away. The world outside Rodez has forgotten me. I work on the inside with the word. I shall write in my own blood or I shall be nothing.

32

Chapter 2

Anaïs said, I tolerate his impossible moods because I'm a woman. If he put his fists in my eyes, I would forgive him for his poetry. It's the inner life I value. His rage is a compensation for the neglect he feels his work has suffered. And Anaïs keeps him on one of the psychological dimensions she uses to accommodate unreal relationships. It's her sense of insecurity has her create a complex system of dualities. For every physical lover there has to be his spiritual counterpart. And my estranged husband, Henry Miller, spends his days exploring Anaïs's sensual mysteries. His music has become the variable orchestration of her bed springs. And his language, 'shit, cunt, prick, crotch, bitch, FUCK', it never modulates in its cyclic range of obscenities.

With Artaud, it's different. His rage is directed against the realism from which Henry creates. Artaud's metaphysical subtleties, the essentially wounded sensibility he brings to life, like an animal hunted out of the forest, leave him brutally exposed to the hedonistic world of the senses in which Henry delights.

While Henry might spit gristle on to his plate, and not pause in talking, Artaud would open his mouth to release a volatile bird, one which would draw blood before flying away, but only out of a sense of frustration at the quotidian. Artaud is always wanting to strip away layers of reality and get to the interior. It's like peeling an onion. He treats every situation this way. He tears down imaginary walls. But there's no way through to the other side. Drugs, madness, he's a human trajectory aimed for Mars.

When a man called, just a stranger at the door, and asked me if I wanted M or O, morphine or opium, Artaud understood. Anaïs thought I was making it up, but a street dealer came without solicitation to my apartment. Artaud saw the spiritual relevance of the incident. Drugs are accomplices to vision. The dealer, in Artaud's mind, had been sent. I was to be the receiver of vision. The light had been given to me.

Henry said that I differed from other women in that instead of furs and jewels, I preferred paintings, poems, novels. But paradoxically, he thinks of me as an empty box. Men like Artaud know how to place their thoughts inside me. Henry's machismo comprises brute screwing. Up against a wall, in compromising public places, his kicks come from realizing sex as an immediate impulse. I'm the ripe fig he enters after having laddered my silk stockings. With Artaud, orgasm is achieved through psychic illumination. He'd rather attain the thing mentally than physically. He fears parting with his sperm, believing it will be used by manipulative occult forces. Drugs are his form of spiritual masturbation. They enhance his inner discourse with the body, that tortured instrument on which he tests his work. Artaud's words are turned on his body like knives.

Henry doesn't know that Artaud visits me. Anaïs would scratch out my eyes. But he finds shelter with me for an afternoon or evening, or he will come by without calling in advance, his clothes dishevelled, his body thin as a bamboo, his hands wrestling with each other, but his eyes so visionary and full of light that one forgets his tormented gestures, his suffering frame. His demands are few. He needs to share his inner visions, externalize them so that they take on imaginative embodiment. Once, when he visited me, he was ringing a large bell. He told me he used it in the streets to warn people away. He was carrying the disease they feared: vision. He wanted to emphasize the ostracism that comes of being a visionary in a material world. Writers, he would say, excluding Baudelaire, Lautréamont, Rimbaud and the surrealists, were representatives of the commonplace. Unable to exchange one reality for another, they set themselves the task of depicting a two-dimensional world. For him, as for his visionary predecessors, poetry represented a journey of discovery, an arrival at a place uncharted on any map. But the discovery entailed intense solitude, and rejection by those who feared the contents of the unconscious.

What I remember of my life is the blazing conflagrations surrounding love. Henry's sadistic rejection of me, the sensuality I experienced with Anaïs, her sense of touch reaching me in places a man would never find, and the casual pick-ups, men and women, both lighting a trail of whisky and recklessness towards burnt-out dawns tasting of sex, ashes, the routed sheets. Artaud doesn't make life ugly, he suffers at the expense of those who subvert poetic truth. When I read the manuscript of Henry's *Tropic of Cancer*, I was vehemently outraged. 'It's not me,' I shouted. 'It's not me he's writing about. It's a distortion. He's incapable of seeing me. He thinks I live in delusions. He perverts everything.' And they said I was hysterical. But Artaud understood. He reached the damaged places in my psyche, the areas that comprise an individual's solitude. The blue desert as he called it. Everything in that locality is mirage. The self, others, the multiple fictions that act out their own autonomous narratives. Artaud wanders in those broken places. His life is devoted to a study of the interior. If he was to draw up a map of his findings, the cities, watering-places, labyrinths, plateaux, jungles he visits would have to be invented.

Once, when he arrived and sat down by the open fire, he told me of how he had been assassinated the previous night. He opened his shirt and showed me the reopened wound. What I saw was a black crust, a scab picked into the shape of a star. He told me the pimp had found him again, only this time it was on the steps of the Louvre. He described the man to me: short, dressed in black leather, and wearing dark glasses. He had removed the dark glasses, and his eyes were gold. They had black crosses for pupils. The man had stabbed him, saying, 'I reconfirm that you are the chosen one.' And Artaud described his immediate death. He had found himself at the entrance to a tunnel. A messenger had told him to advance to a room that must have been used by a car-park attendant. The floor was littered with cigarette-butts, blackened by oil stains. He had felt displaced, terrified by his abandonment. But as he sat there, listening to reverberations which reached him from the tunnel, so the walls and floor turned bright blue. No one entered the room to question him or offer advice as to what was expected of him. He could hear traffic, but he was on the other side of time. And as he sat waiting, so a voice reached him. It said, 'Go back to the world. Madness is truth. You are the chosen one. You will crawl on your hands through the streets of Montmartre, but the word will be written on your back.'

On pronouncing that, he tore the shirt from his body, prostrated himself and asked me to read the word.

There was just a blank back, the spine's curvature knotted against the thin flesh. His fingernails dug into the carpet. I told him the sign was too abstruse for me. That I wasn't its right interpreter. I insisted that I had seen it but couldn't translate its occult meaning into secular terms. In Artaud's vocabulary there was no distinction between inner and outer realities. His difficulties came from expecting people to realize his fluent interchange of values.

What this man wanted wasn't humanly attainable. 'Fear is poetry,' he would say. 'The visceral is an impulse in touch with the metaphysical.' And if he loved me, and in the course of the years he declared his love for most of the women with whom he came into contact, then he never expressed the least physical demand. He had a way of making a woman feel guilty that if she entertained the idea of a relationship with him, she would betray him. His innate fear of promiscuity was, I suspect, the reason for his defensiveness. The body he committed so openly to his work, was an instrument he edged away from sexual contact. He was like a spider when he sat in the chair, contracting, contorting, expanding as his voice took issue with his projects: theatre, the hope of another voyage to Mexico,the books he planned to write, the whole jumbled mosaic of fragments which seethed in his mind without ever finding rest. Artaud lives in a mental dust-storm. He wants to notate the violent multiplicity of thought rather than isolate the particular. He works spontaneously or not at all. Ink won't travel at the same speed as thought. This is his problem.

His feelings for Anaïs were complex. When I had arranged to meet her one day at the American Express, she talked constantly of him. Artaud was the black diamond constant in her mind. With Anaïs there's an exuberance, an immediate up when she meets a new person, but this went deeper, bits of this man had got into her nerves. It was the time she took me to the ladies' room, got out a pair of sheer black stockings and insisted that I took off mine and put them on. She wanted to experience the visual sensation of watching me apply a thin mesh of silk to my legs. It was a moment of intimacy heightened by the awareness that we were in a public place. Anaïs applied perfume to the backs of my knees, so that the scent would live with me as a personal ambience. And she was excited by the prospect of various loves. Artaud had taught her the notion of superhuman love, a union that dispensed with the physical. He wanted her to marry him in her mind. To renounce all dependence on sex for kicks. He hated the idea of Henry and all the others who rippled inside her undulating body. Artaud conceived of a new anatomy. 'In revealing all this to you, I have perhaps killed myself,' he had screamed at her. But that day she was convinced she should follow him. Artaud had invented the name of a country which he claimed would materialize if they went in search of it. He believed that, somewhere in the East, the place would be restored to him. The right combination of psychic energies would afford access to the frontier. Once inside, Artaud was to be received as the deathless one, the intermediary between the states of life and death. Anaïs would be there with him, or so she believed.

This was her way of kicking back at Henry. And it was also her attempt to reconcile me to the fact that she was conducting an open affair with the husband from whom I felt increasingly estranged. Anaïs has the omnivorous appetite of someone who wants everything and gets it. But her psychological constructs play one man off against another and another, so the effects are those of unconscious ricochets, a self-perpetuating spiral of psychic collisions that leave her nervous about meeting each in turn. She confuses minds and bodies, the confessions of one with the fetishistic needs of another. Henry goes for bottoms. I can't see Anaïs walk in one of her tight skirts without imagining Henry slashing the back zip and having his way. A woman on all fours is his idea of sex. Male domination. 'Tie and gag her,' he would say.

Artaud wouldn't be interested. His relative asexuality comes from respect for women. With men he may be different. Or does he invent the possibility of his homosexuality to account for his fear of sexual contact with women? Does he come and go from secret assignations? A meeting underground in Paris? Does his ravaged body respond to a man's lips and fingers? Does he inject his rage into equally tormented orgasms, his body tied and whipped in a closed room?

I imagine Anaïs surrendering to bondage. A violet silk blindfold, her wrists handcuffed by her knotted silk panties, her skin written on by a red lipstick. It's an image that comes back: Henry writing obscenities on the cheeks of her bottom. And in my own madness, I imagine making love to Artaud, his penis is black with a gold tip. In the foreplay he has little flickering fangs extending from his cock, which excite my clitoris. These are my fantasies. Don't we all imagine having sex with our opposites, the figures to whom we never could make love?

38

But I'll tell you a story. I have so many. Some are true and others imagined. I forget the distinctions. After my fourth bourbon, I'm somewhere else. Artaud treats all my stories as realities. Henry disbelieved. He tried to catch me out. I told him my parents were Romanian. He took me to a Romanian restaurant and watched my confusion over the food, the language. But my story?

Every woman at some stage fantasizes about what it would be like to be a prostitute; to earn money, and yet appear to have indefinite leisure. To be an object of continuous desire. For a whole month I entertained the belief that I was a prostitute. I wore a short skirt, a revealing chiffon blouse which gave the outline of my black bra, I balanced on violet suede high heels, my mouth could have been a diagrammatic flourish from Matisse. Each day I took the Métro to Pigalle, stood around the entrance to the station, or walked provocatively through the small alleys. I learnt to walk by rotating my hips, so that I wiggled. And men followed me. I appeared not to hear if under-the-breath solicitations were made to me by passers-by. And if a man was persistent in following me, I courted the danger, the thrill of having stimulated him by my walk, before I went back to the crowded street or lost myself in a store. I wanted to be remembered. I wanted some transient moment in my life to leave an imprint on a stranger's mind. A day, a month, a year from then, he would think how he would have liked to possess me. I was the one who had got away. He would tell a friend in a bar how tight my skirt was, and how my lips were polished like a black cherry. I wanted to become mythic: the woman all men desired, but never had. They would superimpose my face and body on their wives and girl-friends.

And this acquisition of eyes grew to be a need. I would take home my trophies and pour them into a bowl. Green eyes, blue eyes, brown eyes, grey eyes, hazel eyes, black eyes – I heaped then like marbles in a dish. All the eyes I had extracted in the course of my wanderings. And once when a man slapped me on the bottom in passing, demystified me by his physical contact, I committed his eyes to acid. I blinded him in the privacy of my flat. I asked that women should prove invisible to him, so that no matter how much he enjoyed them, he would never be able to see the body of the woman to whom he was making love. And it would grow to be a torment. His hunger would increase in proportion to his frustration. But mostly I was left alone. Men assumed I was too expensive for them or else disinterested. The flirtatious rotation of my bottom was perhaps intended for a lover's caresses. And so my days grew to be the acting out of a part.

At this stage Artaud entered my story. It was towards evening. A smoky blue afternoon sky marbled with clouds arched over the city. I was in a state half-way between inner dialogue and attentive observation of a shop-front, when this man appeared in front of me. It was his eyes I noticed first. They were set back into inner space. The body was emaciated. He looked like an ascetic or a drug user. He didn't belong to the crowds, his sense of reality was clearly a different one. But despite his dishevelled black clothes, he wasn't a vagrant. His air was one of deep sensitivity and refinement. And he stopped me, only this time I wasn't afraid, for there were no sexual understones evident in his manner. Rather, it seemed that we had to meet, and that something within our psychic fields had brought us to this street at this particular time. I would have stopped in front of this man anywhere.

He was confused. He told me he was being followed by members of a black lodge who disguised themselves as the police. They wanted him, as he had the theorem to truth. He had acquired knowledge never before known to man. He called me one of his sisters. 'If I were not perpetually tormented by the pain in my head, I could get away,' he told me. 'It's the pressure on the back of the neck prevents me from working.' He was at once intimate and diffident. We sat in the Café des Quatre Vents, intense, complicitous, as though we had known each other for a long time. He never once referred to my provocative clothes, to the short skirt I was constantly adjusting so as not to reveal too

much leg. He took this in, and seemed to know the story behind my appearance. He accepted the actor as the role best suited
to expressing inner reality. If I'd been sitting there in nothing
but a pair of sequinned panties, he would have accepted that as
my reality. The name Artaud hardly mattered.

I had heard of Artaud through Anaïs. I had been made familiar with his ravings, hallucinations, the tortured complexity of
his emotions. But here I was, confronting a different person. He
was desperately poor like all those who live from poetry. His
hands shook. Thunder skies travelled across the surface of his
eyes. They shifted from clear to storm with an irregularity which
was fascinating. He was serious to the exclusion of humour as
well as trivia. He made it clear that the involuntary commitment to life, and the greater responsibility of preparing for one's
death, were his singular preoccupation. Creativity was the expression he believed should be given to living. And he treated
me as his immediate accomplice. He wanted a whisky. A second
one. And a third. I was glad to keep pace with his intake. He
was fired by the liquor. He grew distraught in describing his
creative struggle. I remember his words: 'I am vegetating. I can
neither advance nor retreat. I am fixed, localized around a point
which is always the same. To go beyond that, I need to live.
And I refuse to live. The point is that my thought no longer
develops either in space or in time. And what comes out of me
does so as if by chance. I have the notion it's independent of
who I am. And if I expressed myself in terms that meant the
opposite, would it matter? I need heroin to escape this trap.'

As he spoke, he was looking around for a dealer. I could see
that he was used to buying street drugs, that he took the risk of
being apprehended in possession. There was a young man who
kept returning to the street. He stood with his back to the wall
and waited. He could sense Artaud's need. He had become the
centre of Artaud's world. He had the substance to placate crav-
ing. He was visibly poor and on drugs. His eyes found nothing
but Artaud's own ravaged body, as though he had eliminated
the rest of the species. And I couldn't leave him suffer. I got

41

out a bundle of notes from my pocket-book, and placed them in his hand.

He was gone immediately. The young man slipped inside a bar, as though totally disinterested in Artaud's approach. The deal must have taken place inside, for Artaud returned with a sachet of white powder. 'It's a means of slowing the tornado,' he said. It was his private ritual, something that distinguished him from the crowds. And he must have recognized in me someone sympathetic. Could he tell that I too had experimented with altered states of consciousness? He was calmer after he had secured his supply. Heroin was one thing, and opium another. 'What I like about opium,' he confided, 'is that the body of soft flesh and white wood given me by I don't know what father-mother is, under its use, transformed. I become someone else. I live in reality.' His eyes expressed the suffering that drove him in search of drugs, and a defiance to stand by that decision. I kept thinking that this extraordinary meeting really was intended. We were outsiders sharing our thoughts, protecting them from a hostile capital.

He spoke with passionate conviction. The mad were those who dared speak the truth. They were attuned to a different form of reality. He was warm about Breton, and the surrealist pursuit of the marvellous, and aggressive about his expulsion from the group on political grounds. 'Poetry,' he told me, 'is a conflagration. Its language is the vocabulary of authentic vision.' He wanted another whisky. I imagined he would use the heroin later. He was burning up on nerve. His voice would rise from a whisper to a declamatory shriek. People would stare, but the protective circle we had formed round each other was inviolable. I wasn't in the least frightened by his unpredictable shifts of mood. I was his friend without knowing him. We were acting out our moment of time on earth. It was our business and nobody else's.

I can still remember fragments of his heated monologue, lyrical gestures that accompanied his gentle moments. And the latter came as pauses in between his more urgently consuming preoccupations. He was a man set on a dynamic preparation for death. The other things, the little things of life, didn't matter to him. 'I am miserable like a man who has lost the best of himself,' he told me. 'What I seek to isolate and surround, what I want to know at least once in my life, is that point of thought where, having cast off the commonest illusions and temptations of language, I find myself confronting a state of mind which is absolutely naked, absolutely clear and without ambiguity or confusion. The blinding experience which rips through all the layers of reality.'

He banged his fist on the table. The waiter brought two more whiskies. We were getting high in Pigalle, the clouds tumbling on a slipstream into the future. When I looked up, the sky was too blue. I thought I could see through its transparency to a couple sitting at a table up above the clouds. They were screened by a red umbrella. The sun was setting on their lives.

Anaïs, Henry, my other friends and problems were left behind. The universe existed in this man. He could have led me into the fire and I would have gone his way, my skirt caught by red and yellow flames. Artaud's intensity hummed like the space inside a clenched fist. If I'd placed my head against his, I would have heard the Atlantic Ocean breaking across an autumn beach. If I'd looked too deeply into his eyes, I would have seen horses being castrated, statues shifting position, the sea in collision with the sky. I would have seen a man attempting to defy temporal limitations. Someone whose poetry burnt into the abdomen. His voice was nearer now. 'This is why I wish to describe the full extent and the full desolation of my pain which is, I believe, without precedent and without any kind of comparison possible. I am called mad because my vision subverts governments. If you listen to me, you will be initiated into truth.'

I didn't care that my short black skirt had ridden up to the level of my stocking-tops. The obscene comments of passers-by were irrelevant to the universal discoveries we were sharing. What men observed on a crotch level was very different from the vertical axis on which I was floating. Artaud's being was a dynamic of constrained ballistics. 'And what is an authentic madman? It's a man who has preferred to go mad, in the sense in which society understands the term, rather than be false to a certain idea of accepted human behaviour. That is why society has had all those of whom it wanted to rid itself, and against whom it wanted to defend itself, because they had refused to become its material accomplices, condemned to be brutalized in asylums. For a madman is also a man to whom society refused to listen, and whom it wanted to prevent from divulging unbearable truths.'

I listened to the authenticity of a man speak from an unmodified inner voice. He had no need to edit or moderate his thought. And this was his trouble. He wouldn't compromise. He despised the corrupt, those who sacrificed the pursuit of their inner lives to business. He believed that truth was answerable only by the systematic elimination of all political intrusion on the individual's inner freedom. He attacked language that was used to validate an ideological lie. He wanted to go back to the more primitive roots of shamanism in which the body is the gestural organism for received inspiration.

He hoped to rebuild his theatre. His Alfred Jarry Theatre and his Theatre of Cruelty had both failed ignominiously. Lack of proper finance, and the extremism of Artaud's beliefs in theatre had brought him into confrontation with the public. He wanted to set fire to the stage, drive the placid bourgeoisie out into the street with their hair in flames. For Artaud, as for Sade before him, theatre was an expression of madness. It represented anarchy raised to the eloquence of poetic speech. 'I give up my fear in the sound of rage, in a directed roaring.'

A cold wind was frisking the street, turning over the dusty plane leaves. He didn't appear to notice; he would have commented on it had the wind been inside his head. And without ordering them, there were suddenly more drinks. It was as though all subliminal wishes materialized in his presence.

Each time I crossed my legs, I felt the sensual friction of silk come alive on my skin. But it wasn't physical desire I felt for this man, it was fascination at his difference. This was the per-

44

son who had told Anaïs that it would thrill him to crucify her. He had claimed that, between them, there could be a murder. But I didn't sniff potential violence in him toward individuals. If he had been strait-jacketed at times, it was due to his rage at a system of things that allowed so little room for individual expression.

What Artaud wanted was a poetry that incorporated danger and concerted action into its field. He chewed on his cigarette. He bit it in the urgency of his speech, and when it snapped free, he crushed it like an offending insect. He was visibly at odds with his body clock. He resented the passing of time, for he would like to have strangled the moment, wrung its neck, and extracted from it the meaning of his pain.

A sailor lurched towards our table and wouldn't go away. He was unpeeling a wad of notes from his pocket. He wanted me at any cost. The bulge in his pants was like a papaya fruit. I wouldn't allow him to break into the hypnotic train of our speech. He was stroking himself in his torment, his eyes fixed on my black-stockinged legs. 'What's the price of some fun, darling? Take me upstairs and I won't ship out in the morning.' He kept on and on with his urgent solicitations. He was clearly English and half drunk. 'Whadya dressed like that for, if you're not a tart?' His demands were growing to a form of salacious incantation, and the waiters did nothing. Perhaps they were taking revenge on me for having seen me day after day casually patrolling these streets, indifferent to all advances. Or perhaps they were frightened of the sailor's confrontational stance.

Artaud appeared not to have heard or noticed the man. He was entirely focused on the inner stream of thought to which he was giving expression. He was telling me of his struggle against the fixed academic conception of theatre, and how lack of spontaneous fluidity both in the writing and the acting of plays had given the public the notion theatre was dead. It was he declared, 'a neuter activity, a subject for café gossip. Theatre is a donkey which has swallowed its own cock'. He was aggressive, spitting with vehemence. I imagined if he stood up, the sailor would make a quick exit, but then he was gentle again, talking about the mauves, greens and oranges that distinguished a particular mood in the late afternoon sky, and comparing it to how women dressed on the boulevards. 'Like flowers, in perpetual sexual motion.' I loved him for that. This man, who spent so much time in the dark crystal at his interior, could still notice the beauty of women crossing Paris.

The sailor wouldn't back off. And having pushed the issue this far, in living out a fiction, I wasn't going to retreat. I could have placed my coat over my legs, but that would have been a concession to macho posturing. The part I knew I was acting was being taken literally by this wolfishly hungry sailor. His erection was telescoping to pop his buttons. This was worse than anything Henry would have staged in public. And if Artaud was conscious of what was happening, he chose to ignore it, or considered it gratuitous to his train of thought. He was talking about the necessity to devaluate written poetry, and the need to emphasize the spontaneous text. 'Written poetry is valuable once, and after that it should be destroyed. It's a question of knowing what we want. Let the dead poets make way for the new. Respect petrifies us.' I could feel the silent anger within him. I wanted him to keep on speaking, so that his words would exclude the sailor. I hung on to his speech as though it was a rope supporting me from a vertiginous drop. People at the bar were looking out half amused at the sailor's obstinate sexual demands. And when people are amused or curious, they remain detached spectators. No one was going to come to my assistance. They must have been secretly hoping that I would get up from the table and lead the sailor off to my apartment. They would have attached their eyes to my bottom, all the way down the street, imagining how my legs would go back over my head at the sailor's demands. They couldn't know that my intentions were radically to the contrary. That I wanted to dematerialize, find myself back in my apartment, safe in the complicitous dark of my bedroom.

I wasn't expecting the violent scene which ensued. Rather like

46

a snake closing on another in diminishing circles, Artaud had waited. With electrified impulses, he got up from his chair, smashed his whisky glass on the pavement, and seethed at the sailor for his disrespect of the conversation. His rage was directed at the man's interfering with the spontaneity of his thought. 'Do you know who you are interrupting? Antonin Nalpas. The chosen one.'

The sailor was too shocked to respond, and too drunk to offer an offensive. He rocked back on his heels, hands reaching out for support holds. Artaud's explosive temper had blown the man out. I fumbled in my bag for money to take care of the drinks, and we left, Artaud immediately taking up his stream of consciousness without reference to the incident.

I put on my long black coat to cover my tiny skirt. I was quickly sobered into resuming a non-acting part. I was an expatriate walking across the city with a thin man dressed in black, whose landscape was a constantly changing interior. I was glad of the racing clouds. A woman's green scarf worn with a violet suit seemed to affirm the aesthetic sensibility which pervaded the city. My attuned nerves could pick out scents in the crowd. Chanel No. 5, and Joy by Jean Patou. I could feel how the woman in me needed attention. Henry had no sense of that person. But this stranger was aware of the ambivalent issues of gender and the subtle permutations of sex that were interactive between a man and a woman. I tried as we walked to imagine him in a dress or a skirt. He wouldn't have been in the least shocked by my drift of thought. We got through crowds guided by the magnetism of his voice. We could have been anywhere. Artaud's inner life was surfacing from timeless dimensions. He was dragging out archetypes. They emerged from him as mythic embodiments which steamed on contact with the air. The statues recognized them. I could feel their snake hair frisk my shoulders, and sense their beady eyes fixed on the shock of the present. Artaud was waving his hands in the air, his gestures appealing to an imaginary audience. His speech was leaving behind him a trail of externalized monsters. And there was beauty

47

too. An April peony would escape from his lips when he talked about the possibilities of finding an ideal love. He was searching for a sister. Someone who would lead him through life, guide him over the cracks that appeared in his mind, the black holes that threatened to suck him across space. Rage was his means of counteracting extreme vulnerability. Cued up to defend his highly individualized vision of life, he tore the heads off all suspecting opposition. There was a panther under his skin, rippling to shred its prey. And given the monomaniacal ferocity of his views, I could understand his falling out with André Breton. Artaud had spoken of it earlier. Both men were sympathetic to madness as representing the most valid form of creative experience, but Artaud had been there, and was still there, whereas Breton had skirted the perimeters in search of poetic imagery.

'Imagine this street trashed by some final ending,' he was saying. 'It's time that the imaginative were afforded retributive vengeance on the masses. What would the bureaucrats do? Die memorizing their credit. I'd like to see THE END. Androids combing the rubbled streets. A death to the old orders.'

We walked rapidly, I doing my best to keep up on my high heels, and he fired by the stimulus of his ideas. We were crossing a bridge, a second and a third, and I could find no guiding landmark. There were lovers on every bridge. A girl's dark-red lipstick being textured into her boy-friend's searchingly oval mouth. But I continued in the wake or at the side of this man's urgent need to reach an invisible point. He might have been headed for a location in a Max Ernst painting.

At some stage I realized that we were not far from my tiny apartment in the rue de Rivoli, for I recognized a tobacconist's, a café, a lingerie shop, familiar places that were part of my immediate locality. I was saying to him, 'Henry loves me imperfectly, brutally. He desires ugly, passive women.' I found myself crying, despite the crowds, the deepening violet in the late afternoon sky. I could hear a blow inside my head knocking me across the bed in one of our vicious marital brawls. The diffuseness, anonymity, indifferent isolation of faces in the street hit in at my solitude. I was suddenly over-exposed, caught in a spot-light which pinned me to a cold blue wall. I was frozen into my obsessive trauma of being left alone for life. I would be found dead in my high heels, the room full of red roses. My histrionic gesture at the end would assure my name lived on in the private mythology of friends.

Artaud knew where we were going. He kept turning round now, suspicious that he was being followed. He wanted my assurance that I would draw the curtains, unplug the telephone and not answer the door if footsteps were heard on the stairs. He whispered to me that if he takes heroin he seals off the routes of access by which his adversaries get into his head. 'They always come dressed as the police. One of them opens his mouth to speak, and his tongue is a bulging sea anemone.'

He pulled us into a doorway and stood there shaking. It was either withdrawal symptoms or fear of someone he had seen in the crowds. He couldn't speak. The muscles in his chest and legs were spasmically contracted. He put his hands over his eyes, as though shielding himself from inner detonations. I steadied him until the terror was over and we got back to my apartment. He was calmer there, sitting in the blue room in which I spent so many solitary, meditative evenings. It was as though he had nowhere else to go anyhow, and that his meeting with me was intended to provide him with temporary refuge. He had already established a microcontinent on which we existed independent of the world. I could have been anyone, but I wasn't. I kept trying to imagine why he had singled me out, and if it was the sensuality I combined with self-deprecation which had appealed to him in the spontaneous moment of meeting. Or did he simply take me for a sophisticated prostitute, a woman in need of conversion to his code of spiritual values? I sat there as a spectator of myself, trying to imagine how he conceived of my presence. His intensity didn't allow me time to slip into the bedroom and change my short skirt, for a long one. I had to sit there, all stockinged legs and high heels, while he directed his eyes toward some inner vision. And he was relentless in his pursuit of realizing the moment through the image it afforded. I felt as though I had been upended and stood on my head in a lake swarming with tropical fish. His ideas beat against the fragile membrane protecting my consciousness. He was talking hurriedly about his plans for another theatre, and his idea of incorporating diverse elements into its possible totality. 'In practical terms,' he was saying, 'I want to resuscitate an idea of total spectacle, where the theatre will know how to take back from the cinema and the media all that which has always belonged to it. But I need money to achieve this. It is now a case of knowing if, in Paris, before the cataclysms which announce themselves, I shall be able to find sufficient realization – financial and otherwise – to give shape to my project. Or we shall see if a little real blood will be necessary to affect my theatre. Assassinate the status quo, and we can begin.'

He slumped back in his chair, exhausted, hands searching in his pockets for tobacco and cigarette-papers. He was unapologetic about his drug need, and treated it as perfectly natural that he should split the tobacco with heroin. He showed reverence for the powder which would give him respite from mental torment. He ritualized the delay. He was asking me whether I lived here alone from preference, or whether as he suspected I was sheltering from a broken relationship. The woman in him was deeply sensitive to the suffering he could see in me, the pain that at times worked itself out from my nerves to the surface of my skin. He said that pain was like a lizard which sometimes needs to sit in the sun. And that this was our chance to capture and evaluate its movements. 'What is it, and where does it go? If we could scrutinize emotional suffering, screen it as we do mismultiplication of the cells, then we would know the meaning of the shadow side of creation.'

He was silent as he concentrated on inhaling. The drug took him a long way back into his head. I could see him repositioning himself somewhere else, his imbalance finding a pivot in mental space. He inhaled a second time, and a third more slowly, deliberately, accustoming himself to the familiar but no less

50

unnerving dimension he was exploring. I accepted it as natural
that I should watch this man be overtaken by his habit. His
immediate euphoria was levelling out, so he appeared serene,
better placed to sit out his inner cataclysms. When he spoke, he
was less like a man instructed by paranoid mania, and more like
someone who has learnt in his dream to balance on the aircraft's wing and not look down. His silences were lengthening.
He made no demands, except to be the solitary inhabitant of
his visionary landscape. His eyes told me he needed me there. I
was the conspiratorial guard he trusted to witness his exploration of a heightened dimension. He must have sensed that I
had experimented with a variety of drugs. He saw no threat in
me. I was happy to watch him go out to an edge and stabilize.
It was so unusual not to be in the company of a man demanding sex. I felt at ease with him, no matter how far out he appeared to be.

As he sat there, uncommunicative, spaced out, I began to tell
him a story, one of the many that corresponded to the various
fictions I allowed myself. I told him of the summer day I went
out to the street in a light summer skirt, my mouth made up to
resemble a dark carnation. I was carrying a lamp intended for a
friend. I saw a taxi waiting outside a bar and got into it to wait
for the driver. Instead of the driver, a policeman came on to the
scene. He pushed his head through the open window and said:
'What's the matter with you? Are you sick?' I told him I wasn't,
and that as the lamp was heavy I had decided to sit in the taxi
and wait for the driver. But the policeman was curious. 'Where
do you live?' he inquired. I got angry and volunteered to show
him where I lived, anticipating precisely what he wanted from
me. He carried the equipment, and I took him to the basement
room where I lived with Henry. Henry was still lying in bed,
wearing a red Romanian embroidered shirt. The table was piled
high with a clutter of manuscripts, books, bottles, photographs,
a pair of my red panties ostentatiously draped over the lamp-
shade. On the table there was a long knife which my friend
Jean had brought back from Africa. The policeman looked over

the contents, smiled, unethically patted my bottom and went back to the street. We were left to puzzle the reasons for his suspicion. Henry said it was the way I walked, and that the man took me for a prostitute. But that was inaccurate. There was something much deeper connected with the policeman's behaviour. I think he suspected that I took drugs, and possibly dealt in them.

I listened to the pause, and then continued to narrate another story. A man knocked at my door. Henry was away at the time. His smile was such that I mistakenly thought he knew me. 'Hello June', he said. 'It's been too long. I haven't seen you since that last time in New York.' And he was already inside, inviting himself to a seat on the sofa. For a moment I thought he was standing in my head. Impeccably dressed in a silver Brooks Brothers suit, a red tie snowed with white polka dots escaping from the jacket, he arranged his hands with the fastidious manner of a card-player. He told me that he had anticipated our date for a long time. He was the man, he claimed, whom I had selected in my head. He had found his way into a dream of mine ten days ago. We had stood by a quay counting the red and green coloured balls that moved in hypnotic circles round a white sky. They were balls, not swallows. He said he had caught a red one and placed it in my hand. But when I returned the gesture with a green one, it had broken open, he said, and inside was a key. It was the key to my flat. He got up and went abruptly to the door. The key sat in the lock and he opened it. With that, he left. He said he had won me, and that we would meet in ten years on a bridge in Amsterdam and be married ten days after that.

Artaud listened with scrupulous attention. Stories like these were perfectly natural to him. He lived for the manifestation of the incongruous. Like Breton, who believed in meetings brought about by occult synchronicity, Artaud was looking constantly for the presence of the marvellous in the ordinary. He was so deeply troubled that I was afraid he'd go into himself too deep ever to reappear. What he had known was bad luck. Buildings

52

fell on him when he walked down the street. Projects were aborted. His dreams were invaded by recklessly malign chimeras. Solitary, fitting into no group, he was a marauder on the outskirts of madness. Heroin was temporarily arresting his panic. His nerve impulses were being cushioned.

He started to tell me about Genica Athanasiou, the woman with whom he had had a relationship over a period of six years. 'When you have managed to penetrate a certain kind of hatred, it's then that you truly feel love.' He spoke like this, always alluding to the incompletion of life, the impossibility of any resolution to emotional need. He told me how he had desired neither to break with her nor live with her. 'Her passion was too demanding. She failed to recognize my purpose. I was the one who was to instruct her in the definitive understanding of life. She saw me as human instead of transhuman. She wanted my balls instead of my nerve linings.' He held off again, living with the suspension of his thoughts, seeing back into a past which was for the moment a reality. 'She was unable to recognize my vocation. I have burnt up a hundred thousand human lives already, from the strength of my pain. She was hurt because I projected our relationship on to universal rather than personal levels. She wanted a metropolitan career. She imagined the possibilities of theatre, she saw herself becoming what she couldn't be – a star. My life was full of negativity. I hadn't realized then that pain, and I mean excruciating anxiety, was the expression of my life. I was trying to avoid the issue. I used drugs differently then. I wanted temporarily to block my suffering. Now, I want to explore it deeper. I go somewhere else to deepen my realization that I can't escape the journey. I can only experience it.'

His speech was becoming slower, more consciously measured. There were visible blanks into which he disappeared, like an aircraft chasing through one cloud pocket to another. He was turning the white of his substance, a man reading himself on the inside and the outside, and translating himself into a chemical experiment. I told him a little of my own pain, and how Henry and I wanted different things in life, couldn't be together, and yet suffered intense jealousy when apart. I kept away from the subject of Anaïs. It was too complicated. Her refinement found an attraction to opposites. It was the aesthete in her who was attracted to Henry's natural state of squalor. Wherever we had lived, he had succeeded in turning the place into a tip. His sprawl of papers, books, girlie magazines picked up on the quays, used cups, glasses, the whole ephemera of living, were dumped as an unconstructed collage on the floor.

I communicated something of that, and he wasn't unreceptive. My human struggle wasn't lost to his concern with the metaphysical. And if he guessed that Anaïs was the third person in my story, he never asked me to confirm it. He listened. And I brought certain of my obsessive threads out into the open, feeling in my own mind that it really wasn't his concern, but that he would listen, for he was grateful to be here, anywhere that provided a refuge from the vicissitudes of the street.

I told him little things. How I loved the woman with whom Henry was involved, and how her love for me superseded her love for either her own husband or mine. And all the time I felt like I had let a dangerous animal loose in the room, one that I could never again retrieve and confine to the sanctuary of my head. I told Artaud of how my life was in fragments. I was in love with the woman who was having an unashamed affair with my husband. If I'd killed them both, I wouldn't have been free. Henry had claimed that our love was simply the prolongation of a habit. He said he had outgrown me but was unable to renounce me. I communicated this to Artaud's brooding silence. I told him that I was plotting to run away with Henry's plaything, and that both of us would take our revenge on him by making his penis redundant. It would be the ultimate humiliation, a form of psychological castration. Artaud was in support of this. He considered the penis as the communicating instrument that prevented men from loving women. 'The new species will be a degenitalized one. People will have sex through telepathic impulses.' He had seen it all in a vision. And my love for a woman found favour in his eyes, as it didn't involve generation.

I found myself losing caution. The creatures I had let into the room multiplied. There was a menagerie of lions, tigers, snakes, vultures. I began to confess to more intimate things. My female partner excited me in a way that Henry didn't. With the latter, it was all brutally demonstrative passion without the subtlety of a woman's tongue to instigate and sustain orgasm. Henry reduced a woman's body to a vehicle for fantasy. I never knew whom he was making love to. It could have been Anaïs, a woman in a short skirt he had glimpsed in the street, a prostitute with whom he'd been the week before. He was never monofocused. He was seeking the woman I could never become. And when I told Artaud that I thought the male orgasm was frustratingly incomplete compared with a woman's holistic pleasure, he was in agreement. He found fault with his own sex because he believed men impregnated women with masculine ideals, and so never allowed them to develop a future on the principles of feminine thinking. 'Women,' he said, 'are supposed to sleep with the butchers who create war. The red-handed who kill and expect sex in return.'

He was a friend. I watched him monitor his inner experience. He perceived every little nuance of change that occurred within him. His body was beginning to crumple with involuntary relaxation. The drug allowed him no choice but to let go.

I continued with bits of my narrative. I was in search of what I couldn't find. A new, fulfilling life. A metamorphosis. I wanted to bundle my pain into a holdall and leave it outside in the street. I saw myself standing on a beach in Italy, a dark-blue sky curved above me, my green scarf making easy gestures in the wind. My lover was waiting for me on the balcony of a white hotel. I would go back there and drink a wine which tasted of dreams, surprise, autumns that reddened dramatically on wild skylines.

For the moment, I felt closer to Artaud than anyone I had ever known. Pain had removed him from the stereotyped convictions of his own species. He was someone living in an intermediary state between the two genders. He attached no importance to his sex. He was concerned with truth. The evaluation of experience in its absolute sense. His ideals were impossible. He wanted to alter a world that was incapable of recognizing the values by which he lived. And for his journey to exist he had to record it, write it down, express it through painting, give voice to it as a broken text.

He was beginning to withdraw deeper into himself. The drug was taking over. I listened to my own story and realized I was now talking to myself. Artaud was inert, staring into himself and not out. The night had arrived outside. I got up to draw the curtains. There was a woman standing in the window opposite. She was wearing a red bra. A man appeared behind her, cupped her breasts in his hands and simultaneously extinguished the light.

Chapter 3

When Artaud first came to Rodez, years of semi-starvation had caused his physical condition to deteriorate. He had been a patient at Ville-Évrard, an asylum in the eastern suburbs of Paris. They had diagnosed him as a paranoid psychotic. His hair was cropped close to his skull. His behaviour oscillated between drugged passivity and a mania characterized by physical violence. He had grown a beard and come to identify with Van Gogh. He was solitary. He avoided contact with the other inmates. He felt humiliated by the condition in which he found himself, and it was this sense of wounded dignity that contributed both to his illness and his sense of a future in which he would regain his freedom. He was preoccupied with reformulating his identity. He attributed his sense of frustration to a conspiratorial plot in which he was the victim of almost every social class. A persecution that extended to a psychic plane. Artaud was engaged in a spiritual struggle to subvert the satanic forces that had continuous access to his mind. Like Rimbaud before him, the conflict was as much physical as mental. He would claim there was blood on his hands from the conflict. A blood he could never erase.

And what do I tell you? A psychiatrist's observation of his patient comes about mainly through discourse. Like everyone else's, Artaud's mind was a mass of contradictions. Sometimes I faced a man who welcomed a sympathetic discussion of the arts in terms of psychological reference, and at others I was met by someone who would have strangled me, had the opportunity presented itself. On one occasion, Artaud must have punctured his skin prior to our meeting. He came to my office with blood standing out like red war-paint on his cheeks. He had caked his mouth with it, and the result was a crusty, black lipstick. We neither of us mentioned his behavioural aberration. I treated his departures as realities, and by doing so I defused his potential for irrational rage. No matter his situation, Artaud never lost his sense of theatre. The dramatic was his natural form of expression. His emotional field was one of high voltage. When he spoke passionately, his nails bit into his palms. He wanted to lacerate all pretension, horsewhip the literati for their separation from the work. His savagery lay in his viewing everything as extremes. There was fire and fire, and no intermediary territory. His sympathies lay with the mistreated – the poor, the mad, those who pursued art as a total commitment.

We were in the Unoccupied Zone. Artaud's hunger had led to his eating rats at Ville-Évrard, and under my care he began to put on a little weight. He claimed he had the formula for a deathless existence, and that to achieve this state it was necessary to live outside the body. Some days he presented himself to me as Nalpas, and on others as Artaud. Or he was Poe, Baudelaire, the Comte de Lautréamont. He came to my office carrying a dead rat in his mouth, the creature suspended from his lips by its tail. He would smoke his cigarette the wrong way round, inserting the glowing tip between his teeth. And once he punched eye slits in a pillowcase and sprang on me as a masked intruder. I had to separate affectation from spontaneous dementia in my assessment of his character. It wasn't easy. An asylum is a closed universe in which obsessive behaviour patterns, neurotic compulsions, the involuntary adoption of multiple personalities, violent expression, all manner of deranged conduct becomes accepted as natural discourse.

What I wanted from him wasn't so much a sense of compromise as one of balance. He needed to bring his imaginative reality into alignment with the external world. Some sort of integration was necessary if he was to function on a competitive plane. Artaud's world was defensively monocentric. He expected others to perceive the singular importance of his inner discoveries, and felt victimized at every expression of difference.

Artaud saw madness as an initiation. He thought I should conduct my work with him as a ritual, the developmental process leading not to integration but the realization of mystery. He told me that the rainbow would appear from his mouth when we arrived at revelation. He liked to show me his hands which he believed had turned gold. And his eight remaining teeth were oracular mountains, summits on which the breath was apotheosized into prophetic speech.

What happens if I don't personally like someone? As a psychiatrist I'm supposed to desubjectify my dislike of a face, a mannerism, someone's blackened fingernails, someone else's obesity, a voice that's too loud for tolerance, a habit of smashing a fist on the table to emphasize rage. What if I don't like it? I grew to dislike Artaud's idiosyncrasies. His monomania was at times too much for anyone. No matter my professional ethics, I twisted inside myself at his endless recourse to obscenities. 'What the fuck am I here for?' he would endlessly repeat. That was only the beginning of a remorseless attack on every aspect of living. He wanted to renounce his body and yet retain the privileges it afforded. I developed an antipathy to the burn-holes that spotted his shirts. In front of me, he would use his cigarette deliberately to score craters in his cuffs, collar or shirt-front. I was trained not to react in the interests of his safety. I let it go. But then I came to dread this aberration, and I wished sometimes that he'd set fire to his shirt, his jacket, his hair, and sit there as

59

a crackling human torch. I can still smell the singeing and see the black discolouring circle expand to a hollow eye in the cotton fabric.

I had a woman patient who refused to tell me her fantasies unless she sat in my lap to make her confession. She would position herself with erotic expertise and place her head on my shoulder. She had done this with her father, nearly always on park benches, and the fixation had remained. She believed herself to be an actress. She had good clothes, cashmere skirts, fitted jackets, a variety of silk blouses and scarves, and applied her make-up with skill. Artaud avoided her. He was convinced that she was in the pay of an occult bureau. He would refuse to come out of his room if he caught sight of her in the corridor. He began to send her a series of intimidating spells. Using drawings of signs and layers of coloured ink, he would streak the paper with his blood and inflict cigarette-burns on the finished product. The result was a semi-obliterated text, but one which menaced by reason of its occult implications. This woman, called Denise, became hysterical on receipt of each of the spells. She would run outside into the asylum grounds, arms raised to the sky, imploring protection.

Artaud was unrepentant. He refused to lessen his attack on his terrified victim. He was convinced of his right action. When I asked him to desist, he simply angled his cigarette in the corner of his mouth, an idiosyncratic gesture of defiance, and refused to speak. This contraction on speech was a characteristic act of contempt on his part. It could last for days, and at such times he'd write me letters making demands for heroin. Only by using the latter, he claimed, would leakage be prevented from getting into his head. I had to threaten him with another, more intense course of electroshock therapy, if he continued to threaten Denise. It was my only level of appeal. And it worked. Artaud made one last extreme gesture, painting a pentagram on the outside of Denise's door. I had the latter transferred, for Artaud's mind was consumed with threat.

On the morning Denise left, helped by a nurse into a waiting car, I found Artaud hammering on a large drum in his room. He was registering the fact of her departure. He said that his release would be imminent now, as the source of possession had gone out of his life.

I thought of Denise, huddled under her black coat, being conveyed not back to her family in Paris but to another regulation hospital. And my purpose? To go on exploring inner frontiers, investigating psychic realities which alienated my patients from rational human discourse. Did I really believe this? I had to let Denise go in the interests of safety, but my emotions were not without a feeling of loss. The repressed erotic nature of our meetings lived on in me as an alerted need. She continued to assert a hold on me, and to fuel my sensual fantasies.

Artaud was different from the other patients at Rodez, in that he systematized his psychosis into a form of creative structure. I encouraged him in that. I treated him as I would a friend. I had him strait-jacketed only when he attempted to bite me, or when he intended physical violence to others. There really wasn't any hope of a cure and I wasn't looking for one. I was trying to help him to adjust. His visions were illuminating in that they lit up an area of experience I associate with poetry. Reading a poem should be like discovering a bit of consciousness we never knew before. In other words, the interior, with all its jungles, lakes telescoping to the centre of the earth, lions carrying suns on their backs, people flying, the magic universe we associate with metaphor. In this respect my beliefs, encouraged by the surrealists, were in accordance with his own. Good poets want to re-create the universe.

Artaud tore at his subject-matter. He treated his writing like someone eating meat with their hands and tearing it off the bone. He was rightly impatient with formalism. Breton had blown convention to the sky. Chirico, Dali, Ernst, Tanguy, each had exteriorized his subjective universe on the canvas. It was the only way forward. I was excited about the possibilities that Artaud was exploring in his fragmentary texts. He was treating the paper as a surface to be attacked. Writing for him wasn't a means of modifying or falsifying experience through the medium of language, it was the chance to communicate direct with his sense of outrage. It was a form of primal anarchy. If we all communicated without the selective process of language identifying with thought, the world would be reinvented. It was what Breton wished. A reorganization of the psychic chaos which had come to be manipulated by ideologies. And as a psychiatrist my life involved the constant analysis of inner states. My patients, including Artaud, neither wished to be a part of the system, nor had any practical means of entering it. Part of my job was to make these confined individuals feel less isolated. By identifying with their particular states, I became witness to their discoveries. I went down that road. If there was a disembowelled tiger lying in the dust, and further on a man hanging upside-down from a tree, holding his detached head in his hands, I had still to go on to the ruined château, knock at the door and be received by a man no bigger than a mouse who was to conduct me on a journey through the basements.

I visited so many places. I listened to those who imagined they had murdered. I acted as a confessional to one who was sure he had created the universe. There was no end to the hallucinated states in which people experienced imaginary lives. Should I have been attempting to reverse the order, and have them switch over to what we conceive as reality? I lost myself in their narratives in the way I did when I was writing a poem. I felt I was experiencing the truth, no matter how bizarre its revelations. And I was privileged in that I was the objective ear to their fantasies. I could learn from the process which they were living out so intensely as to be blinded by the content. Their revelations became the material from which I could construct poems, or work up in my journals. I used what came to me in a creative sense.

But I couldn't do that with Artaud. His experiences were so individually internalized, and so curiously linked to a direct source of creativity, that they were immediately recognizable as his own. 'Baudelaire,' he told me, 'did not die of syphilis, he died from

the absolute lack of belief attached to the incredible discoveries
he had made in syphilis and repeated in his aphasia.' This as a
digression, almost a parenthesis between a diatribe against psychiatrists and rage at his being prevented from taking the train
to Paris. Illness and creativity. As a psychiatrist who is also a
poet, this is my subject. Artaud pathologized the creative act.
To him it was inseparable from disease. I looked at the notes I
had made on him: 'Transformation of the personality, of his
official identity. His personality is split. Entertains ideas of persecution with periods of marked violent reactions.' I objected to
his spitting at me. He claimed this was a reflex action to dispel
evil. His constant humming and spitting were impenetrable bar-
riers he erected in order not to connect. His obsessions seemed
incurable. My job was to try to get him back to sustained literary composition, something I assumed would focus his psychic
energies.

There was the additional problem of his violence. Artaud
couldn't be allowed to return to civilian life. He was a danger
to himself and others. Ever since he had lost the sword he had
received in 1936 at a voodoo ceremony in Cuba, he had been
convinced that he was a target for assassination. He had to be
prevented from lighting fires in his room as a form of protection. He would tell me that when the sword rematerialized he
would castrate me on my desk.

On other days he saw himself as the victim of a publishing
fraud. He had the idea that his little book *Le théâtre et son
double* had sold half a million copies in occupied France. He
wrote abusive letters of demand to the publisher, which I prevented from being sent. I remember that one of them was written in rat's blood. The use of rodent's blood was in his mind
the most toxic form of curse that could be placed on a designated individual.

I was anxious that he should return to work, but he complained of being continually exhausted. He would spend his days
in bed, smoking, or else he would hammer on a large drum. He
was in the process of going to ruin, despite the additional weight

he had gained, so I decided to give him a course of shock treatments to help accelerate the process of rehabilitation. Without this course of therapy I considered Artaud would be too mentally confused ever to regain his creative faculties. His sporadic genius was unfocused.

I had attended a conference in 1938 on the benefits of electroshock treatment to patients suffering from schizophrenia and epilepsy. It was an Italian doctor, Ugo Cerletti, who had first made the connection between pigs being given an electric shock to the frontal lobes to subdue their panic before slaughter, and the possibility that it might reduce symptoms in the violently disturbed. I was willing to entertain the risk of possible failure. But there was a shadow that troubled me. This was the little known case of Friedrich Hölderlin. Soon after the initial symptoms of what was thought to be psychosis, he was given a form of primitive shock treatment, his eyes concealed by a blindfold, his mouth gagged. The terror of this ritual precipitated his mental deterioration. But those were early days. I was confident that the new, much improved treatment would be beneficial to Artaud. I had to dismiss the case of Hölderlin from my mind. The yellow pears and roses splashed in the lake's reflection together with swans had come to form an imaginary topography in my mind whenever I recalled his poem 'Hälfte des Lebens'. I was standing there in the burnished autumnal glare, not thinking of the man who had written this poem as a premonition of madness. After writing it he spent the rest of his life playing disconnected pieces on the piano, managing once a year to scramble a few fragmentary lines on the page. It was Robert Desnos who told me this. It was a well-kept secret. I was confident that the same wouldn't happen to Artaud.

Of course I had to face him with my decision. No anaesthetic was applied. The patient was strapped down, a spatula placed in the mouth, and electrodes attached to the frontal lobes. A short jab of current was discharged through the patient's brain, causing immediate and delayed convulsions. A coma followed, and the patient was expected to experience memory loss, and in some cases periodic amnesia lasting over a period of months. I considered the facts. The treatment was a new one, and arriving on the tail end of the furore surrounding surrealism, it seemed still another experiment in the parapsychology of the creative mind. I couldn't face Artaud in his present condition. I owed it to him to try to restore greater clarity to the inner chaos in which he would always live. Poetry as I had experienced it is a form of controlled madness. It differs from psychotic hallucination in that the poet selects imagery from a sensitized unconscious, externalizes it and retreats. The patient is unable to depathologize symptoms and has no alternative world into which to escape. Subjective reality was becoming for Artaud a blinding mirror. And he had come to confuse his reflection with reality. He needed to swim through the mirror and discover the swimming-pool at its interior, and from there go on to the other side. I wanted to break that glass and increase his awareness that things existed independent of him.

Artaud had almost ceased to bother with perceptual images and lived solely through imaginative ones. The death-wish in his psyche was constant. He gravitated towards dissolution and was obsessed by his evacuative products – excrement and urine. He had phases of storing both, jealously guarding his ejecta from the nurses for fear they would use it in occult preparations. I feared he would regress to an incurable state. As an anarchist and poet, I felt I could meet Artaud half-way. I was sympathetic to his belief in a private mythology having more importance than an inherited ideology, but Artaud had lost the power to manipulate his inner chaos. He was in the process of being savaged from the inside. The rage he projected at social conventions was in part generated by the increasing sense of paralysis he felt at being unable to convert his negative psychic energies into a recognizable framework. In my clinical work I had never treated anyone with quite so intense a degree of suppressed rage as Artaud. There was little which didn't conflict with his sense of affronted identity. Any attempt at modifying his habits was received as massive antagonism, a policy that extended to drugs.

65

He was endlessly requesting opium or heroin or peyote. But chiefly opium. I refused him drugs, but friends brought him in various substances, and I didn't object to their use. I met him on whatever level of reality he entertained.

Opium brought him release from sustained mental pain, but it exacerbated the pathological lethargy about which he endlessly complained. I kept him away from speed, knowing that it would amplify his persecution mania. It wasn't easy. As a proponent of surrealism and experimentation with automatic writing, I had come to support Rimbaud's belief in the systematic derangement of the senses. I was predominantly interested in the relationship between madness and creativity. Artaud was too much on the side of madness, and I had to shift him back to a level of creativity, extrapolate his rage, so that it burnt on the page. I wanted him to subvert internment in the way Sade had done, building outrageous fictions to compensate for confinement. Would any other psychiatrist have used the example of Sade to a patient? And I had him read the Marquis, no matter that I risked exciting his autophobic propensities. Was this irresponsible? I don't think so. The unconscious contains the contents of a book before receiving it. Everything is in there – psychopathic dementia, incest, the day we walk out on childhood and make our way towards the château in the woods, the initiation ceremonies in which we go blindfolded through the dark, the loves, wounds, complexities, the deaths we experience in broad daylight, while we're driving, out shopping or taking the dust road to a farm where a dog is barking at the sun. A dog that would like to swallow the sun and run with it in its belly across the white fields. I had to show Artaud the way back. He was trapped face up against a hallucinatory prism that extended vertically to the sky. Artaud was beating his fists against the glass. I could hear him. The sound reverberated night and day.

I was confident the treatment would be painless. The actual execution of it I put in the hands of my research assistant Jacques Latrémolière. Artaud liked the latter and had spent a considerable time engaged in metaphysical discussions with him. Both men had pronounced mystic tendencies, and I hoped Artaud would accept the treatment as a stage towards illumination. I was on the side of innovation. Artaud wanted to be respiritualized. Early experiments with shock treatment had proved successful. But there were casualties. Abnormally long periods of coma subsequent to convulsions were one of the detrimental findings. Cerletti had ruled out the efficacy of injecting the spinal fluid of electroshocked pigs into his patients.

I wrote to Artaud's mother. She was anxious that we should proceed. She feared that her son's condition would never improve unless some form of radical treatment could be found.

Artaud demanded that, if he was to undergo the ordeal, he should be handcuffed. He insisted he was a criminal being led to his execution. He wanted six white roses to be placed on his body while the treatment was being administered. He wanted someone in attendance who would read the Upanishads to him. If he came through it, his memories of the experience would be oracular. It was his way of making me pay for the possible failure of the experiment. And how else could I view it but as a possibility which might or might not work? Would I be faced by a different Artaud? Would thirty electroshocks transform him into a functional being? I let it go. I had poems to write, other patients to see, the onerous commitments implied by being the administrator of an asylum. Rodez. It was the death of me.

We began treatment in June 1943. Latrémolière noted that Artaud was suffering from chronic hallucinatory psychosis, with polymorphous, delirious ideas leading to a doubling of the personality and the belief in a bizarre metaphysical system. He responded well to the first treatment, although he proclaimed himself a deity on returning to his room. From the second session on, he complained of back pains. He experienced a bilateral, constrictive pain which was augmented by the least movement. Even coughing caused him to convulse. He adopted a bent-over walk, his thorax protruding in front. It was difficult to ascertain what was affectation and what was directly attributable to the treatment. The complexity of Artaud's intellect confused any issue demanding truth. And from the third session on he became violently opposed to the therapy. He came to equate it with torture. He was convinced that he had died under shock coma. He claimed to friends that after one session it had taken two hours to come out of coma, and that his body was already on a stretcher bound for the mortuary when consciousness returned. He wrote me endless letters appealing against the treatment. He complained that the agonizing existential crisis of coming out of coma and being unable to orientate was an insufferable dilemma. He talked of dissociation and partial amnesia. He feared turning into a blank, a black-suited 0 who would be placed in an egg-cup, his skull shattered by a spoon.

But our clinical findings were encouraging. Artaud no longer spent all day in bed smoking and repelling invading presences. In a letter asking for the treatments to be discontinued, he wrote that he no longer believed that he was being persecuted, and that he saw nothing now but the paper on which he was writing, the people, the trees, the surrounding neighbourhood and the blue sky above. It was encouraging. I took him off the histamine injections he was receiving for back pains and decided to support our initial success with an increased course of electroshocks.

It was summer. I had him sit outside in the grounds whenever he could be persuaded. He didn't care what century he was living in. The war? There wasn't one. His deprivations consisted of the things for which he repeatedly asked his mother: chocolate, walnuts, hazel-nuts, jam, cheese, figs. He thought his mother was deliberately denying him the provisions he requested. We had cerise peonies lolling on their stems, foxgloves acting as speckled trombones to the bees, indigo campanulas, pink and white petunias, bushes loaded with smouldering red roses, but he took little or no interest in the external world. He paid no attention to the martins feeding at dusk, their shrill, streamlined bodies performing undulating aerobatics above the gardens. This was a point on which Artaud differed from Breton. Breton was concerned with beauty: the colour of a woman's eyes, the dramatic tones of a thunder sky above Paris, the physiognomy of a sculpture, painting that celebrated colour within its imaginative content. Breton's preoccupations differed radically from Artaud's concern with decay. Breton had at one time walked through the streets of Paris with a rose in his hand, the reddest he could find, searching for the face who deserved his gift. Artaud would have despised such a gesture. I tried to heighten his awareness of the external world around him. I wanted his inner world to find an opposing tension, and hoped that his energies would address the two dissonants with his own voice. Instead, the investigative arm of his poetics extended only to his own pathologized psyche.

That summer we sat outside. I liked the sultry evenings, the martins grabbing aerial plankton, and the plane trees beginning to meditate in their cobalt shadows. After working all day with the obsessed, the psychopathic, the psychotic, my mind was anxious to return to my first subject – poetry, and the permutations it had undergone since the first wave of surrealism had broken over Europe. I never mentioned my own writings to Artaud. I kept away, sensing the combustible antagonism that would arise from my mentioning the subject. I felt he was sure to accuse me of tapping his psychic sources and interfering with his creative process. Artaud never praised his contemporaries. His admiration was for the dead: Poe, Baudelaire, Lautréamont, Rimbaud, and of course Van Gogh. He felt comfortable with those who had suffered. The living were seen as conspirators in a plot aimed at deposing his rights to be the chosen one.

Poetry and medicine. I served both. Artaud's output prior to internment was small. His reputation amongst a cult circle depended on the theory he outlined in letters. I wanted to shift him back to the thing itself. His creative gifts were being obscured by inertia. If the complex was a biochemical one, I was confident that a further course of electroshock treatments would restimulate his neurology.

We sat. I tried to direct his eyes towards the red involuted peonies, but without success. I could make no reference to the

69

anticipated sexual pleasure I would enjoy later with my wife. Artaud had no interest in the erotic. He would begin by telling me that his hallucinations had dispersed, but that he knew he was under spells placed on him by the Sûreté Générale, the British intelligence service and the Vatican's Congregation of the Index. Before being transferred to Rodez, Artaud had sent telegrams to Hitler. I insisted that his mail was inspected before dispatch, as I didn't want a political scandal on my hands.

I suffered for Artaud, although I did not share his belief that he was the victim of demonic possession. He would claim every evening that nicotine and heroin were vital to a healthy constitution, and that only these could restore vitality to a body damaged by occult traumatism. I had given him as a present a copy of Ronsard's *L'hymne des daimons*, and he was anxious to talk of his discoveries while reading the text. He spoke of the cabbalistic conception in the poem, the discriminative contention between light and dark, and how daimons are provisional and inanimate entities who find life in imitation and serve as doubles of the angels. He was sure that Ronsard had like him suffered acute mental torment. He believed that Ronsard had fulfilled his purpose as a poet, which was to translate into humanly accessible emotions the workings of the absolute.

I couldn't get him to accept a lesser role for poetry. He was preoccupied either with spirituality or obscenity. There was no middle ground. I couldn't get him to talk about Paul Éluard or René Char, to name two of the poets I admired, nor on to the fiction written by Louis Aragon, Philippe Soupault or Michel Leiris. His inner eyes were too attentively open; I wanted to unlid the outer two. Artaud had grown to be autophagic. His was an organism feeding on itself. Eventually there would be nothing left of him. His weight loss was a metaphor for that process.

But we were sitting outside, and I was temporarily distracted by blue lobelia and red geraniums turning dusty in the summer air. The scent of the earth never failed to exhilarate me. It was like reinventing childhood through smell. I had come a long

70

way. I wondered what I was really doing here working as a psychiatrist when I would have preferred to spend my days writing. I had become one of the many who stand on the platform conscious that the train they are taking is heading in the direction of compromise. I should have been on the one departing for unknown countries, forests in which human skulls sat like owls in the trees, and rainstorms deposited sapphires on the path leading to a hut in which the dead were being interviewed. I had to pursue that journey in the hours when I wasn't engaged in my profession. For a brief hour at night I would look out of the jolting carriage window at jewelled boa constrictors basking in a circle of naked women, or I might see a poet standing with his palms held up to the sky, magic writing appearing on those upturned hands. I needed to acquaint myself with that landscape each day. It was a confirmation that I was living.

I tried on various occassions to revive Artaud's interests in photography. I wanted him to dress a cane in cabbage leaves and make something of the image, but he refused on the grounds that the idea contained a concealed eroticism. He had a mystic theory that Satan may have used cabbage leaves in the creation of the feminine vulva. He saw all libidinous intentions as conflicting with his idea of degenitalized man. It was impossible to shift him from the mystic ramifications that existed in his mind. He had his own system of creation. Who was I to attempt to disprove it?

Yet the shocks were making him marginally more sociable. Before that, he had been too prickly to approach. He even spoke one evening of how much better he had been treated at Rodez than in the six or seven asylumns in which he had been kept before coming here. I was encouraged to continue with a treatment that appeared to be having beneficial effects. His back pains had decreased considerably, and there was a greater sense of animation about his person. I was planning to edit a series of books from Rodez and requested that Artaud translate a number of chapters from Lewis Carroll's *Through the Looking Glass*. There was a young surrealist painter from Marseille, Frédéric Delanglade,

71

at Rodez, and I thought it would stimulate Artaud to suggest a collaboration. Carroll was no stranger to Artaud. I knew that he had undertaken translations of this odd work a decade earlier, even if it was only for financial reasons. The project started out well. Artaud had little English, so was reliant on cribs from a member of staff. He would show me some of his results on those evenings when we managed to sit outside. At first, he was enthusiastic and planned on doing the whole text. He was re-discovering a concentration that he thought had deserted him. He was getting back to writing. But after a number of weeks he abandoned the project. He grew to have a personal antipathy to Lewis Carroll. He considered that there were too many con-cealed allusions to sex in the book. He considered that Carroll had purposely devised a plot to prevent him from working. He started to compose written spells to exorcize Carroll. He ac-cused the latter of being salaciously antagonistic to his nervous health. I could do nothing. The work was abandoned, to be taken up later in one of his characteristic creative furores.

My relationship with him was such a difficult one. I was first his doctor and second his friend. It was hard to maintain a complementary balance. I couldn't let myself in on his subjec-tive suffering. I had to consider it as symptomatic of a particu-lar psychosis. My job demands reports even if I am one of the most unorthodox of psychiatrists. Artaud was admitted here as a case. As his friend I tried to get him to reconnect with the idea of Paris and his former life there on the fringes of a literary circle. Letters did get through. Artaud's madness had contrived to give him a legendary status amongst a tiny cult. 'When one is shut up, one ends by imagining the outside world does not exist,' he had written to me. I felt discouraged by the results of his return to poetry. Soon after the abandoned Carroll text, he showed me a long poem called *Kabhar Enis-Kathar Esti*, in which he had invented his own language in accordance with his theory of breath and the cabbalistic books he was studying. It was un-intelligible. I believed in every form of verbal experiment, but this was scrambled and inarticulate. He confided to me that he intended to write only in a language of his own invention, for then he wouldn't be plagiarized.

We returned to shock treatment. One of the beneficial effects was that he abandoned the name Antonin Nalpas. He now considered himself to be Artaud again, and so his association with writing was easier to re-establish. I could give him the connection back to his past. He continued to write me appeals to stop the treatment. His savage invective against a form of therapy he considered to be barbaric was interspersed with profound mystic discursions into the nature of good and evil. Artaud had been unable to resolve the guilt he felt at abandoning the Christian religion. He fluctuated between writing encomiums about Christ as a manifestation of light, and declaring that every form of repression in man issued from Christian dogma. He could on the same evening pray fanatically in the chapel as well as abuse the chaplain with insults. It was part of his mania.

And mine? I was writing erotic poetry, which I considered unpublishable because of its content. My imagination was embodying every form of deviancy. It was a private, intrinsic world, not one that I'd developed as a consequence of treating the pathological. Its extremes found a parallel in the erotic writings of Sade and Apollinaire. I kept the work secret. It may have been unconscious desire not to be rejected by publishers that led to my being so hermetic. It was anyhow a time of war, and the chances to publish were fewer. Writing had gone underground, which was nothing new for poetry, but it made the process even more difficult. Besides, I had little time for anything except the care of my patients. At night I would run my finger along a shelf of books and wonder who amongst the names was still alive. And what becomes of the imagination? Do we telescope into it at death and encapsulate ourselves in a dynamized idea of consciousness? I don't have the answers: I can only imagine the possibilities.

I was often disquieted about my own health. I tended to overwork, and stress interrupted my sleeping pattern. I would sit up with my pulse racing, listening to an uneasy roar that

73

seemed to come from the skyline. The sound couldn't be located. It was somewhere and nowhere. It was either the war or the sound of blood beating too loudly in my veins. I would look at my wife sleeping beside me. Even after all these years of marriage she would go to bed with the spaghetti straps down on her black silk slip. I liked to kiss her shoulders, and it was a prelude to our love-making. She never forgot that favourite gesture. But in these intense, panicky moments, nothing helped. I was over-exposed to the unknown terror. I was forced to confront my fears and know them for what they are. I came to understand psychic reality as myth. I came to terms with what I conceived as a psychological polytheism. Our images are our great passions, and the mythological arena that comprises our interiority is one of unresolved conflicts. I told myself these things, but in the face of real mental disorder nothing works. No amount of theory reaches the psychotic. My dilemmas were panic crises, cracks in the earth, but not earthquake fissures.

What was encouraging was that Artaud seemed happy to want to be himself again. Paranoid delusions were still a part of his behaviour, but he no longer felt it necessary to invent his identity. He even wrote to me about his desire to instate a link with his past. 'In my present state, what will do me the most good is to re-establish contact with the things my confinement has made me forget.' It was certainly to be the way forward, but Artaud's health was fragile. Several times we had to treat him for internal haemorrhages. He had spent his life abusing himself, and his continued use of whatever drugs he could get, didn't help. I managed with Frédéric Delanglade's assistance to get him painting. Artaud had come to like this young painter, and he found much in Delanglade's powerfully subversive expression to feel encouraged to take up that medium himself. I believed that a patient's selective images when externalized serve as a form of therapeutic traffic between madness and reality. I hoped that painting would serve as a corrective means of self-discovery for his confused state. For despite his repeated requests to be returned to civilian life, there were uncomfortable digressions in his behaviour which suggested that delusions persisted. He had taken to writing letters to Hitler, and dedicated a copy of his *Le théâtre et son double* to the latter. He was also writing letters to Pierre Laval, the president of occupied France, requesting that he intercede to have him released. Artaud was still asserting that he never had been mad, and that his arrest in Ireland was a conspiracy on the part of the English people. He told Laval that if his sword was returned, he would legislate over world affairs. Of course I stopped these letters, but they were indicative of his state of mind. He had written to Laval that he had in his own opinion never been subject to the least trace of mental disturbance.

I had tried unsuccessfully to locate Denise. The situation demanded care. I couldn't be seen to be abusing my professional status, but her glow continued to live in me. Her red suits, her excessively high heels and mannered walk broke into my reflective moments. I began to imagine her surrendering to me in a hotel bedroom. She would sit on my lap, as always, strategically pressurizing my cock, and this time my hand would slip beneath her skirt, while the other began undoing her blouse. She would gasp as I disengaged the left breast from her black bra, and began erecting her nipple with my tongue. Convulsive shivers would electrify her spine as I found the places between her legs which had her arch her back and cry through her open mouth. She would get up from the bed and wriggle free of her tight skirt. Then she would come at me, lips working to engorge my cock, fingers igniting the pleasure points in my testicles. A repressed nymphomaniac would surface as she tongued me juicily. Worked up, and wanting to avoid immediate orgasm, I would flip her over and give her the oral delicacies for which she was ready. My tongue would create an erotic calligraphy on her clit. It would be like running my taste-buds over and over the purple skin of a ripe fig. And having made her delirious with an oral vocabulary, I would enter her, feeling her legs go up high, and then close over my back, her tongue dancing with mine in an interlocking mesh of fire. Her body would be sinuous and undulating, her fingers expert in the places where she incited response. It would be a long and modulated journey to orgasm, Denise's voice ascending scale after scale of desperate pleasure. My back would be lacerated by her nails, my voice inarticulate at the suspended moment of crisis.

I drifted in and out of these erotic reveries. It was always her figure that dominated these involuntary interludes. Denise with her green suit, Denise in a baggy black jumper with an art deco ruby spray pinned to one shoulder, Denise wearing a monocole and black lipstick, Denise in black panties. . . . It was hard to let the visions go. They filled the gaps I had between seeing patients, and the lapses in concentration that occurred in conversation. I was anxious to have news of Denise's progress. In my mind I could already see the hotel where we would meet, its windows open on the dark-blue Adriatic, a girl in a red swimsuit standing at the water's edge, lifting her hair up with a clip preparatory to diving in. Denise and I would sit out on the terrace at night, basking in the uniform heat, listening to the waves build and collapse, peak and expire, white susurrating hands extending their fingers around the world.

Even in the warm night she would be wearing gloves as a dramatic gesture. She would remove the red satin covering finger by finger and place her left hand in mine. The dominant one in love-play, the right hand would be unveiled only when I stripped her naked. Before kissing me she would drink a glass of cool wine, and then impart its fragrance to my lips, my tongue. Her red lipstick would leave the most subtle coating on my mouth. Every action would lead in this delayed manner to the eventual crescendo. Each caress would be like mounting another stair towards the bedroom. My hand would begin by brushing her cleavage. Hers would lie lightly on my thigh. I would insert a finger between her breasts, but slowly, ticklishly, as though a fly was trickling across her skin. Imperceptibly, and by agonizingly suspended movements, her hand would come to rest on my lap. With her eyes placed on the horizon, she would trace her little finger over the outline of my erect penis. No one would ever suspect what she was doing. And I with apparent disinterest

76

would move my hand to her knee, let it rest there as though the gesture was one of companionship, before beginning my gradual ascent up one leg, pausing to encounter the warm thigh, then tracing the lightest touch over her crotch, one finger lifting the elasticated triangle of her panties, and feeling her whole body jolt with excitement.

I imagined this. One of the few sanctuaries we have as humans is the private space in which we locate thought. How could my patients know that I was preoccupied with salacious fantasies? I had the right to play my little games, and I indulged to the full my erotic imaginings.

Artaud started to make charcoal sketches at my instigation, mostly faces and revelatory signs. I had prepared the way for the creative attack he was to make on painting in the coming months, the intense, implosive passion he was later to bring to that medium. But he was still predominantly concerned with occult warnings. He claimed that groups of people were meeting in Paris to cast magic spells, and that they came together in houses in the vicinity of Notre-Dame-des-Champs, the Porte d'Orléans or the Porte de Versailles, the Cimetière Montmartre, Père Lachaise, Les Invalides, etc. And that when they were at work, police stopped the traffic for hours and the invisible dead became apparent to those who could see. Artaud's loathing was directed at the bourgeois, the middle-class cattle as he called them, whose material work ethic obstructed the imaginative ideals in which he believed. No amount of treatment could dislodge his belief in the potency of spells.

It was about this time that I received an extraordinary revelation from him in one of the letters he was in the habit of sending me or to the other resident doctors. 'The French people have forgotten,' he wrote, 'because they are under a spell, that I have answered their occult practices with piles of bodies right in Paris, and that the streets where these corpses are littered have been closed off by the police to allow the road-workers to collect the dead and clean up the street, a fact that everyone has deliberately forgotten so they can indulge in the luxury of believing that life is going on as usual despite the fact that I am depleting the population of Paris and the universe.'

I could accept this on a metaphoric level, but Artaud spoke factually. I should have liked to discharge him, but I couldn't risk the possibility of his being arrested by the police. Outside Rodez, he might manifest Hitlerian sympathies, or begin preaching in the streets. And anyhow he had no form of income and no manner of supporting himself.

The war was dragging painfully to an end. Rationing was austere, but we managed somehow, largely owing to farm supplies from the neighbouring villages. In a very real sense there were gaps in all our lives, and I too experienced a strong sense of having lost touch with reality. The war had arbitrarily fragmented all sense of continuity. I carried on with my work. I am a doctor before all things. I need to tell myself that.

A trickle of friends began to visit Artaud, and I gave permission for him to go out in the town accompanied. His ravaged body was conspicuous for its being so thin. 'I am a fanatic, not a madman,' he had written in one of the letters it had been my duty to monitor before sending out. Being amongst sympathetic friends helped to control his violent eruptions against society. There was something about his condition that saddened me deeply. It was perhaps the essential incurability of his state. No amount of analytic discourse was going to free Artaud from paranoid delusions. It was the isolation of his insanity which he had recognized. Unlike some of my patients, he was able to measure his subjective pain against a potentially objective state. Madness was an intolerable condition because he could empathize with its opposite. I have seen so many cases for whom inexplicably there is not the least chance of adjustment to social norms. And as a poet I have always asked, what is this chemical imbalance, this apparent multiplicity of selves, and why is it that from birth some are confused with inarticulate realities, psychoses that relate to no form of external reality? As a doctor I have researched the pathology of mental illness, I have observed how the unconscious enters into each mental act, I have attempted to psychologize neurotic phenomena. But I have no answers to the causal effects that transmit madness, other than an awareness of chemical anomalies which may contribute to an individual's behaviour. And Artaud? Where is there a beginning or an end?

Before I let him go I insisted that his friends provide financially for him, and a trust was set up from the sale of paintings and manuscripts auctioned in Paris for this purpose. I placed him under a less rigorous psychiatric regime at Ivry. He was to live alone in a pavilion in the grounds. That was the practical side of affairs. Artaud left Rodez for Paris like a man expecting to be acclaimed as a fascist dictator. I dreaded the right-handed salute, but it never came. He thanked me for my part in establishing him as the chosen one.

That was Paris. A freezing station. A patient, a friend being met and dispersing into the city night. I had work to do. His old blue second-hand suit had a tear above the left elbow. I remember that. The tear widening as he raised his arm. Artaud back in circulation.

Chapter 4

What does anyone do to occupy their days? There's no conceivable way in which we can count our thoughts. There are too many, and they are too transient to monitor. People compute money around the clock, but who has ever tracked the number of their thoughts into the billions of misappropriated ideas they become? All of the concepts, images, involuntary flashbacks and flashforwards, the seething trivia, obsessions, preoccupations, the blanks in which there is nothing, where do they all go, and what do they mean?

I drink to erase the hurried traffic that streams through consciousness. And soon I'll go back to New York, for my life with Henry is over. His compulsive infidelity and his indomitable ego have forced me out of his life. He expects me to wait patiently until he tires of Anaïs. I am to be a spectator in the assuagement of his libido. And I am bored, disapproving, charged with animosity over the negligence I feel. Henry sees himself as a verbose genius; I view his mind as saturated in the pedestrianism which informs the self-assertive male. They are everywhere.

Men who assume their sexuality gives them importance. A woman has only to walk down the street in high heels to attract their uniform conventionality. Perhaps this is why we prefer to give ourselves to the shy and unobtrusive. It's the quiet men I favour, those who can attune to their own and a woman's feminity. Those who feel no need to impress by posturing.

Today my mood is ten shades of blue, graduating from cobalt to a tonality close to cornflower. Mostly it stays at the cobalt end of the spectrum. I listen to Billie Holiday's slow, elegiac vocabulary of loss. Her voice comes at me from the bedroom, a woman speaking of the intimate scars that love inflicts, her timbre bruised by alcohol and drugs. She is my accompaniment in the blue hours. I wear her music like a favourite perfume. Her voice lives as a subtle form of possession in my head.

I walked out on my mood to meet Anaïs at La Coupole. Our attraction is predominantly a physical one. I have read too much about myself in Anaïs's correspondence with Henry to be able to meet her on any level of truth. I invent characters to confuse her conception of me. I knew of Anaïs's dream, the one in which she made love to me, and how on opening my legs in her dream my vaginal lips were moving quickly like the mouth of a goldfish lipping the water. In her fantasy I possessed a penis and penetrated her like a man. She had wondered how I conceal it from Henry. The knowledge that she had experienced these fantasies, and I suspected she had imagined rather than dreamt them, afforded me still another fictional role. I was an intersexual in her mind. Together we could experience the voluptuous sensuality of lesbianism, as well as share the rare phenomenon of one woman possessing the other with a penis. I was thinking of this in the taxi that took me to our meeting-place.

She was there, of course, dressed in a coral shot-silk dress, her hair done up in a simple black velvet bow, her legs arranged like two silk flowers. She was wearing the turquoise bracelet I so liked, and her old rose coat with the Medici collar was draped over a chair beside her. She was smoking a black Sobranie, the gold tip reddening to fuchsia where it made contact with her lipstick. Everything about her was stylized, and I had the immediate impression that she must have spent hours making up for our meeting. I was aroused. A woman can satisfy another in a way that leaves a man appearing clumsy. And hadn't Anaïs already described to me her excitement at visiting clubs in which lesbian acts were openly performed for the clientele? She had related to me an incident in which one of the two women had strapped on a large dildo, and after tantalizing her partner, had entered her with the latex prosthesis. Anaïs had described her intense stimulation at viewing this sex act. She told me that when she had returned home, she undressed, lay on the bed and imagined that it was she and I who were performing a similar act. She said she was so excited by the prospect that anyone who had walked into the room could have made love to her.

These are the sort of repeat thoughts that become obsessive associations with a person. I would never be able to think of Anaïs now without living as a voyeuristic spectator to the scenes she had described. There was a cognac awaiting me. Anaïs knows my tastes, and I needed the immediate reassurance of the alcohol to lift me. I gulped at the hit it gave me, and a double was too minimal to get first arousals. I ordered a second. Anaïs just smiled, and then leant over and kissed me deeply on the mouth. Any resistance I may have had, crumpled at that contact. Something of her was being transmitted to me, jabbing impulses that tasted of coffee and the individual scent that lived on her tongue. I was stung by her spontaneous passion. She wanted me to sit next to her, but I took a seat opposite the books and accessories she had placed beside her. I felt so much hostility toward this woman, but her passion ignited me, and her enthusiasm for the creative people in her life was contagious. She was generous in her praise of contemporaries, and never bitter or competitive in respect of their achievements. Nor was she expansive about her own work. She kept that away from me, and if she used it as a psychological identity, it was in the company of her male friends, almost as though she needed to assert her validity in the arts.

Anaïs had lost touch with Artaud, although he counted her amongst those included as sisters of his heart. I felt a need to shield him from her, and a corresponding possessiveness. I disliked the way she claimed men for her own – hadn't she seduced my husband? – and I wanted to keep this important fragment of my life away from her.

I felt her left knee come into contact with my right, tentatively, exploratively, but absolutely certain that it would not be rejected. There was the friction of silk, the warm flesh glowing beneath. A hand playfully followed, but soon withdrew. Anaïs knew that I could do nothing to resist her erotic coercion. She was flirting with me the way lovers do in a cinema. She was alternately sultry and kittenish, confidential and quietly exhibitionistic. I had come here in my black velvet skirt and matching cape knowing what would happen. I felt a degree of tension and curiosity which I rarely experience with a man. It had been the same with my lover Jean. She had provoked in me a sense of risk, a desire to outrage which I had long ago lost with men. I had no intention of going back with her, the brasserie afforded me a sense of being on adventurous but neutral territory. I responded to Anaïs's pressure on my knee by discarding my left shoe and snaking my stockinged leg around her right ankle and shin. All of this under the comparative safety of the table. I ran my toes sensually across the arch of her foot and she replied by kicking off her shoes. Our two feet joined in a union, sole to sole, our painted toes wriggling to establish a sensitizing rhythm.

All the time we went on talking, I stared direct into her eyes, the conversation running at tangents about Paris, the respective cut of our dresses, a particular perfume by Guerlain, the rudeness of taxi-drivers, small things that clutter up the initial anxiety of meeting. She was telling me of the explosive red peonies at Louveciennes, and of the forty scarlet roses her father had bought her on his recent visit. Her father adores her. He chooses her presents in the way a lover might select intimate things for a mistress: silk dresses, lingerie, bitter chocolates, perfumes, an effusive extravagance of flowers. Anaïs never tires of speaking of her father, he is the aesthete who has been instrumental to the refinement she has cultivated in herself. He is the man who might have walked out of Proust into a concert hall.

As our feet continued to explore a sensory rhythm, I told her that I would like to take drugs with her. And more specifically, opium. It wasn't Artaud who got me on to this substance, I had used it regularly in Paris as a way of escaping from the ruins of my marriage. I told her it would have to be at Louveciennes, the two of us seated on cushions in the intimacy of her bedroom. She would wear a black turban, and I a violet one.

Of course the idea excited her. She saw it as an invitation to sex, a future date in which we would explore each other's physical desires under the accommodating influence of a drug. Anaïs liked to talk about the erotic. We both shared a taste for yellow-cover fiction, those novels which are sold on the counters by the Seine. She delighted in talking about *maisons closes*, whips, garters, black stockings, provocative panties, alcoves, mirrored ceilings, peep-holes, the whole gamut of sexual stimuli. When she wasn't engaging in sex, she was fantasizing about elastic positions, unusual combinations involving more than two people. It was one of our café subjects. It would have nauseated Artaud, and Henry would have spiced our dialogue with crudities and destroyed the subtle fictions we never tired of inventing.

Anaïs was telling me about how excited she grows when she is massaged by an Indonesian woman. The woman goes further than the dictates demanded by body massage, and spends a long time working on Anaïs's breasts and bottom, trailing a slow finger along the divide in her buttocks being the masseuse's signal flourish that the session is over. She then wraps Anaïs in green towels and sends her into the bathroom to get dressed.

Our heads come closer together. I know she is enjoying the fact that people glancing across from nearby tables surmise that our periodically whispered tête-à-têtes involve sexual confession. I feel her hand on my leg and I draw the chair closer to the table. The circular motion of her fingers is making progress under my risen hem. She reaches my stocking-top and plays with the red suspender strap. Then the hand goes to the inside of my leg and makes a sensual return to the pivotal knee. I drag at the remains of my lipstick-stained Gitane, and Anaïs signals to the waiter for another cognac. Her mouth is like a red lily. I want to force my tongue into its corolla, but I refrain. I'm jolted too by the thought of how many times she must have practised fellatio on Henry. The same mouth. She would divorce emotions from eroticism, but with me it's different. I'm more fragmented than she is, less focused and privileged in my direction in life, and less able to view sex as an exploratory adventure for kicks. Anaïs is looking for my complicity in the areas she intends to explore. She thinks that because I'm married to Henry, I'm easy game. She assumes that I too tolerate his going with whores and endorse his attitude that women are conquests to be entered in red ink on a score card. It's this thinking that has her read into me the idea of a woman who does anything for sensation.

Who am I? I let the question ride. I return Anaïs's exploratory caresses, my left hand going up her skirt and working across the bridge of her crossed legs. She blows blue smoke at my lips, and surrenderingly uncrosses her legs as an invitation to go higher. I leave this gesture in reserve and come back down her legs, watching her laugh as she senses me place the hem of her skirt level with her knees. And so we begin all over again the subtle moves in this under-the-table courtship. Our sensations are heightened by the risk. She picks a dark carnation from the glass on our table and places the maroon flower to my lips. She says it matches my lipstick, and how she would like to run it along the length of my spine. She would like to give me a dry bath in bruised rose petals, and where they stuck, pick them from my skin with her lips.

No man has ever told me these things, and with the heightening effect of my third double I began to wonder if I shouldn't go back with her to Louveciennes and experience the delectations she would impart with her expert tongue. Some of the pain in me was starting temporarily to evaporate. I could feel the displacement occur in parts of my mind. It was like that feeling of flying in and out of the clouds before the plane gets up above them. I was being jolted into luminous blue spaces, intensities of light which I thought no longer existed in me. Being with Anaïs was often like flying, no matter the hurry with which she left one person for another in her restless search after truth.

She must have had a hunch that I was in contact with Artaud. She disliked losing people. It made her feel depleted if people drifted wide of her magnetic centre. Artaud had rejected her and she had never forgotten it. He was one of the few whose solitary vision had no need of her aesthetic discourse. Nor could she offer him money. His contempt for material things made him intractable of her wishes. And his violence, while it may have fascinated her at first on a theoretical level, left her terrified. But she was still in love with the romantic conception of the poet as madman – Artaud carrying a bell through sleeping Paris, stopping occasionally to shriek a curse on the living or to kick the bodywork of a parked car. It was an image to which she returned. Anaïs thought in terms of archetypes. In her thinking, the poet was a shaman, a man whose spirit power communicated from the dead to the living. He conformed to her idea of someone possessed by creative delirium. She saw him spitting hot coals out of his mouth as he dreamt, or battling with a giant snake on the stair. What I didn't dare suggest was that he possessed the dangerous vision which she would have done anything to acquire. Anaïs's retreat was always into the recognizable safety of art. Artaud rejected the latter, and treated his work as a violent reaction to conventionality. I suspected that he hated every aspect of art. And Henry, who was forever on about Rimbaud, attempted to emulate the latter's hatred of bourgeois comforts but lacked the young poet's hallucinated senses. Or maybe I was being bitter. I didn't care. The little I had seen of literary life in Paris gave me no incentive to pursue its doubtful élite.

Our feet and hands continued to do outrageous things under the table. We both adopted an expression of indifference to the pleasure imparted. And that was greater for the anticipation and the impossibility of our consummating the act there. I had planned to get away quickly, but neither of us was able to part. We were locked into timelessness.

With the feel of Anaïs's five painted toes alive on my silk-stockinged foot, I began to tell her a story. I don't know why. I wanted to go somewhere that would make her jealous of my temerity. I needed to discover for myself if the narrative was true or false. I forget so much when I drink that I have constantly to rediscover the events of my life. Novels come from this sort of confusion, but writing has never interested me. I prefer to talk. I like to coat my words with whisky or cognac. That way they come out at blood heat.

I placed a finger on Anaïs's pouting lips and said, 'Listen, I want to tell you a story. It happened six weeks ago. It was two after midnight in Montmartre. Henry and I had just had one of our blazing rows. But brutal. Things were said which were unforgivable. Words on which there is no coming back, for they strip the psyche bare. The whole flat was reverberating. It was suffocating.'

I felt the expertise of jabbing in a pin as she winced, her feelings divided between her love for Henry and her sympathy for me as a woman. Despite her erotic appeal, I wanted to nail Anaïs to the reality of pain, that emotion she consistently avoided by running back to her husband as soon as the flames grew unmanageable.

'I went out to the street, my tension so great I could have screamed. But I didn't. I started walking, oblivious to the drunks who tilted toward me, the gangs who hung out on street-corners. It was cold. I could smell the river's dark green coat. In my mind, I was headed for a specific house. I knew it without having any knowledge of the district. It seemed to me that if I kept on walking for fifteen or twenty minutes I would arrive at my destination. The house was distinguishable by the fact that it was painted a jay's-feather blue. I knew that when I reached the street in which the house was situated, a man dressed in a ballet dancer's sparkling tights and a black eye-mask would be standing outside the front door. He would neither acknowledge me nor turn me away. He would hand me an envelope as a sign I could enter. These things were written into my mind. It was like another way of seeing. The immediate external world of familiar observations had disappeared. In its place was this other indelible landscape. I ran part of the way, my high heels clattering down the narrow, cobbled streets. A man ran up a window and called after me, "Hey, do you want a bed for the night, sexy?" but I was already out of his range and headed for a night he and his neighbours would never know.

'I travelled through the dark protected. I stopped to look at nothing. There were streets, cars, cafés, clubs, zigzags of red and blue neon; a couple kissing in a doorway, I remembered her floating white skirt, and further on two transvestites were touting for trade at the entrance to an alley. The tall blond one was dressed in a feathered skirt. These were images which jumped out at me, but they were no more than incidentals in passing.

'And do you know, it was like having different eyes. I was in an unknown Paris. My problems with Henry seemed to have taken place hundreds of years ago. I kept wondering how such a short interval of time could have removed me so totally from the events of my life. I had sobered up in the night air. I found myself laughing out loud. For the first time, I felt free. And of course it was there. I didn't have a name or a district by which to cross-check my instincts, but I knew I had arrived at the street I had to reach. The house was half-way up the street on the right. The man dressed as a dancer was waiting at the top of a flight of stairs. There was a light on in the attic. The house looked like a ship sailing the night seas.'

Anaïs's foot froze in its sensual rhythm and I could see that she was arrested by my narrative. I placed one hand unmovingly on her knee and continued.

'The man came down the steps, handed me the envelope, and without saying a word motioned for me to follow. I climbed the steps conscious that I wasn't dreaming, and when I placed my hand on the stone support I felt it cold from the night air.

I was tangibly alive. When I got inside, he gave me a joint and I followed him up a spiral wooden staircase to the library. Stuffed birds in glass cases stood in alcoves. I was shown into a room in which an olive-faced man with dried-out, emaciated features, his thin shoulders padded by a bullfighter's jacket liberally sprinkled with rhinestones, was standing over a huge book. It looked like he was officiating at a ritual. I have never in my life seen such a large book. It occupied half the room, and its width would have matched a double bed. He and two other masked participants opened the book, and inside fitted into satin moulds were two naked women placed side by side, but each facing a different direction.

'I wasn't sure at first if they were dead or alive. This book might have represented a sarcophagus, layer after layer opening out to present a necrophiliac's index of bodies.

'Strangely enough, I wasn't frightened. I was curious. I wanted to see the three men turn and turn again. I was desperately inquisitive, and quite powerless to assert control over my reactions. In that sense, it was like a dream.

'The man who had led me into the room whispered in my ear, "We're going to participate in various forms of sex." And the officiator at the ceremony was already lowering himself on to one of the two women, easing himself into a comfortable position. His two assistants massaged oil into his back, and I saw to my astonishment that the woman was alive, for she lifted her legs, toes pointing in the air, before closing them round the man's back. I was told that I could make love to the woman whose abandoned body lay parallel to the other. As a sign of desire she had arched her copper legs and opened them out in anticipation of my lips. The whole thing looked like love taking place in a coffin.

'The red warning light in my mind went out. I knew I would never again encounter such an adventure, so I went down on the woman and excited her to orgasmic pitch through the interplay of my tongue and fingers. One of the assistants began to massage heated oils into my back and bottom. The sensation had me undulate with unrestrained need. I was swimming voluptuously beneath the man's hands, my partner licking my breasts and working an expert finger along my crack. I kept on thinking I was dreaming the thing – and perhaps I was – but the pleasure was too intense for what one experiences while asleep.

'I won't tell you everything that happened. There was too much. I went back downstairs led by the same figure in dancer's tights, the impartial observer who watched everything but never participated. The others referred to him as the night-watchman. He missed nothing, so I was told. He knew what went on behind closed doors all over Paris. He slept during the day. As I left he told me to open the small blue envelope. I obeyed, and read the words NEW DAY.

'I hurried back through streets I no longer recognized. The landscape had changed. A policeman asked me where I was going at this hour, each shadow menaced with its dark threat. I didn't know where I was. I ran from street to street, and it started raining. A blinding torrential downpour turned the street to crystal. I was standing battered and breathless from the assault of rain. I didn't know how to get back to my district. I clattered along in my soggy high heels and inadvertently looked up at a house number. It was 83. There was something half familiar about the house with its twenty-four-hour security light burning in the hall. And then I connected. I was in the rue de Rivoli. Barbara lives at 83. I had nothing to lose. I pressed the intercom buzzer and waited. Each renewed buzz was answered by a prolonged pause. Then, coming out of the interior, and I thought it was rain drumming on the hood of an automobile, I heard footsteps. I couldn't believe it. Barbara called out through the letter-box, "Is that you June? I saw you from my bedroom window."

'That's where my story ends. It's a snatch, a fragment in time. But it's a reality. Never again will I walk the night without the memory of what happened in that room with the book open on two naked bodies.'

And wanting to wound her, I added, 'Henry appeared ridiculous after that incident. You know very well that tough guys aren't to my taste.'

I knew this would open a scar in her, for Anaïs, who professed to be the advocate of the sensitive male, seemed to forgo her psychological credo when it came to her choice of lovers.

I stopped talking and waited for the pause. She had no immediate uptake. If there were comparisons she could make from material which fed her clandestine journals, then she failed to make the connections. She was silent. Her inner dialogue must have been saying that I was either a liar or a threat to her as an erotic chronicler.

I watched two shark's fins erect themselves in Anaïs's eyes, then slowly drop back to the current. The brasserie was filling up. People were coming in for lunch. There was a tension in us that strained a seam. We seemed to have exhausted the erotic possibilities available to us in a brasserie. Needing a respite from our complicitous dialogue, I went off to the ladies' room. I stood in front of the mirror and dusted my nose with sparkling powder. There were ladders in my stockings and the seams were misaligned. I took out a second pair of sheer black ones which I kept in my handbag and watched myself consciously delight in the intimate ritual of unrolling the transpicuous silk from toe to thigh, four red suspender clasps maintaining the right tension in each stocking's breadth. I checked there was no bunching at the knees, and that the seams followed the centre curve of my legs. And they are good legs. Anaïs says they are the best she has seen. Men's eyes drop to them. When I wear a short skirt I'm in trouble.

I went back and Anaïs had touched up her face. She was in the process of putting her compact away. She was shy about such things, preferring to maintain the feminine mystery behind these little rituals. She was smiling again, and the tension had drained from her face. The storm had broken, but I sensed that my remark about Henry would be repaid. She ordered another coffee and a cognac for me.

'And Artaud?' she asked. 'What has become of our crazy

Antonin? I hear nothing of his escapades these days. The last time I saw him was in Montparnasse. He was standing on the plinth of a stone lion, his right hand raised in a Nazi salute. He had only one sleeve to his jacket. It would have been comic if it had been someone uninspired. There was a large black dog watching him from a distance, fascinated almost by his theatrical gestures. He was performing a left to right half-circle, scanning an imaginary audience and pitching his voice like someone attempting to control a crowd. The square was empty. He couldn't see me, for he was hallucinating reality.

'When two students rattled past, they turned and stoned him with abuse. "You mad shit. Look at that skinny water-rat. Come on Nazi, give us your salute." Of course he probably didn't even hear their ridicule. He was somewhere else. And at some stage he began this extraordinary dance. It wasn't like anything I had ever seen before. It was a primitive rite accompanied by a primal mantra. Then he started spitting. He was commanding someone or something to keep away. I had to restrain myself from rushing up to him and dragging him out of this public square before the police bundled him off in a van. When he swung round to shriek at the indomitably passive lion, I could see that the back of his jacket was splashed with paint. He must have done it himself. Orange, red and mauve radials of paint had congealed at random on the cloth. I could imagine him treading paint into his jacket, stamping it into a rough texture. Stamping and spitting.

'I stayed a long time watching his solitary performance. He appeared like a witness to the end of things. The thing burnt itself out. His rage diminished.

'I remember how he left the square, disconsolate, his savage exclamations decreasing. He was like a firecracker sputtering to an inconclusive end. Someone trailing off into the Paris evening. Lonely, drenched, unstable. And I kept thinking, who will take this man in? Where will he go? Is there a house for madness? Is it something that we leave in a friend's attic or store in a safe? I asked myself so many questions. I kept trying to imagine his future. Where would he go tomorrow, and the next day? Would they take him inside again? Use a strait-jacket to repress the voices?'

Anaïs looked up. Her story had been almost as long as my own. She was still back there, facing the rain and the mad figure of Artaud gesturing to the city's gargoyles. She must have been able to feel his tension in relating it, hear the ferocious disquisition he aimed at the presences he called demons. He always spoke of the latter as real.

I placed a knee against Anaïs's and let the silence ride. I was taking in the intense green of the mint julep that someone had ordered at the next table. It was the green we never find in plants but wish was there. The young girl in her fashionable black polo-neck jumper was looking at it as she might at a jewel.

'I don't see Antonin,' I said edgily. 'If he comes by then it's because he needs immediate help. You know what it's like. Money. Drugs. Refuge. There's not always anything I can do to help. I don't have that much for myself.'

'But I'd heard he sees you more regularly than anyone,' she persisted. Her thoughts hurried into the corners of her eyes. I could see them watching me like cats.

'I never know where he is or how he lives,' I replied evasively. 'He's another visionary in the history of that sad line who suffer because they live outside society. Whenever I have seen him he's too burnt to talk about anything but his visions. You know these. I don't have to repeat them.'

'Madmen are important to me,' she replied, 'in connection with my own writing. Artaud's special. He rejects help, because what he contains within him is too big to be exchanged in return. He's the least compromising individual I've ever met. He'd rather kill himself than betray his vision.'

'And what is that vision?' I inquired.

'It's got to do with the belief that all truth belongs to the imagination. Henry would like to have that commitment, but he doesn't. But perhaps it's better if we don't talk about Henry. Artaud asks that the practical world admits him with providence, but at the same time fiercely undermines it. Give him the best apartment in Paris, and he'd transform it into an imaginative kingdom. Outwardly, the red carpet would be holed with cigarette-burns, disorder would rule everywhere. Can you imagine the kitchen, the unmade bed heaped with books and discarded notes, the air acrid with hash smoke? Artaud doesn't live in the comfortable structured world he thinks is his due. But we love him for that. He attacks the world for denying him what he would reject. This is the visionary calling as I see it. What he needs he creates inwardly as a system of ideas.

'Most of us can never go that far. I couldn't give up my house, my silk stockings, my perfumes, the intimate dinner parties at which I question the metaphysical absolutes life and death. I couldn't do this on the street in holed shoes, and lacking the knowledge of where I would sleep at night. He does that because he's so deep in his psychic interior that no journey is going to return him to real necessities. And lacking the ability to do that myself, I'm fascinated by the things he discovers in the course of his journey.

'He must have witnessed so much that we can only imagine. Even on a level of seeing the bizarre in Paris. Those who walk across a city at night encounter the contents of fiction. I have known it in my taxi dashes back to Louveciennes. The circles of men who light fires on the river banks, the vagrants, the mad who come out in the deep night. A woman giving herself a miscarriage by jumping down a flight of steps, another walking the streets with her arms outstretched, searching for the man who left her so long ago she can't remember. All those people poking in doorways, garbage bins, exploring the secrets that sleepers put out on the street at night. And over it all the dark stretched like a panther's skin.'

Anaïs was living out her nocturnal findings. I watched her suspended in drift, the images breaking loose as fall-out. She got back to me with a perceptible jolt, and her hand caressed the inside of my knee. She extended her index finger, her direction pointing confidently towards my crotch. I felt a sustained prickle, an excited rush, but she withdrew her gesture and let her hand return to my knee. Her eyes came on big, she let the cigarette-smoke spiral lazily out of her dark mouth. I wanted her, but I wasn't going to allow her to seduce me. I preferred to luxuriate in the fantasy of our making love in her black silk sheets. In my mind, she was depilated. Her pussy would be the pink of a camellia petal. She would squat above me, lowering herself on to my explorative mouth. My tongue would dab like a fine paintbrush forming a textural consistency. Her body would pivot on this one point. My salival calligraphy would quicken in response to her rhythm. She would look like someone on all fours trying to escape herself. And as she moved towards the first spasmic intimations of climax, I would stop. I would leave her arched in a void, pleading with me to resume. And I would. Parsimoniously at first, and then responsively I would place her back in the same agonized delay. Her body would be on the edge of coming, and I would withdraw my darting tongue. She would beat on the bed with her fists, and I would take it up again, go through the motions twenty times before I followed her to her convulsive end. Her buttocks would sink over my face, her hair would scatter red fire across the bed.

I couldn't remember whether I had drunk the last cognac, or how long ago I had given up counting, but there was another glass beside my elbow. Something in me registered caution despite my willingness to abandon myself to getting drunk. Anaïs purposely didn't look at my glass and made no comment on my drinking. I knew she was counting on her sobriety to direct me into indiscretions. I wasn't going to fall for this. Inside, I was like someone locking up a house before going away. I was securing windows, checking doors, cutting off supplies which could lead to fire. My house wasn't going to be forced by an intruder.

Anaïs was looking for the opportunity to get behind my defences. I hoped she would hear the rattle of my heavy keys, the dull inexorable reverberation of a door being slammed tight on a cellar. The black waters of my psyche had risen to the ceiling. She would never find the space to slip inside. But before I went out to find a taxi, I wanted to take dramatic liberties with this woman. And if she never agreed to see me again, what would be lost? Her body was the one Henry had pushed to orgasmic shrieks.

I drew my chair up to the table. The student drinking mint julep had been joined by a friend. They conversed across two tapered emeralds. The younger of the two girls was reading a passage from a novel out loud. They were sharing an oasis at which both had arrived. It was their moment in time, a reciprocal realization that neither would forget, ten, twenty, thirty years from now, the memory would be there, sharp as the taste of raspberries savoured on a picnic in bitter grasses under the high, mottled plane trees.

I pressed my knees against Anaïs's and then wound a foot like a twist of ivy round her calf. I was working toward the divide in her legs. I opened them with gentle pressure and ran my hand up to her V. Her silk panties were moist, soft as the interior of a plum, as I began brushing a fingernail against her jewel. She caught her breath and I could sense the nerves go tight in her body and then slacken. If we had been on a bed she would have abandoned herself with urgency. The sense of risk fired her adrenalin. 'Carry on, darling,' she whispered. 'Make me come surreptitiously.'

We kept up a semblance of conversation. My finger flickered only occasionally, but it was in contact with a restrained tempest. Anaïs kept positioning herself to make access easier for me and to intensify the pleasure that pronounced itself in her protracted shivers. I would like to have held her legs open and tickled her with a pink feather. Instead, I continued to touch her volcanic source. I was orchestrating this woman's fire. I expected the table-cloth and the curtains to autocombust. The beginnings of pleasure are like wind turning over the heads of opium poppies.

I was going to leave her in this state of sexual torment. I touched her where it burnt, and her mouth opened as a red oval. I playfully released a stocking-top from its suspender straps and rolled it to her knee. She was thrilled by my daring. If the

96

table had been pulled away, our erotic activities would have been evident to all. For a moment I contemplated doing this, exposing our intimate scene, and dashing for the door. Onlookers would see me folded in a black velvet cape bundling myself into a taxi, the blue fog hanging in low clouds along the boulevard.

Anaïs was pleading with me: 'Come back and I'll give you everything. We'll be together always. I don't need anyone else. It's always been you. We don't need men in our lives. We'll live together at Louveciennes. My father will support us. June, be with me. . . .'

I withdrew my hand abruptly and backed off, my eyes fixed on her unbelieving expression, my body already out the door, although I was still sitting on the edge of my chair, my hand reaching reflexively for my glass, the cognac burning in a long trail down my throat, its fires registering in the soft tissue of my larynx. The syncopated fragments of everything we had known together flashed up as crazily incohesive nebulae. Anaïs making up her face, our holding hands together under the flowering chestnuts in the Bois de Boulogne, her enthusiasm for Proust scattering lyricism across a candlelit dinner-table, the dangerously edged equivocation of our conversations over Henry, our trying on tight skirts together in a fashionable boutique, and in the process scandalizing the assistants. The whole period of our intermittent time together was loud and vivid as I sat there already attracting eyes to my back, my face, my outspread hands. I could hear the building collapsing in my head. The action belonged to the amplified silence of a dream in which worlds collide inaudibly.

But now I was no longer sitting. My hands were placed on my hips, my high heels were wide of me on the floor. Anaïs couldn't believe this. She was trying to make the transition from intimacy to being confronted by cold hatred. And having once asserted my power, I wasn't going to relinquish the hold I had on this vulnerably displaced woman. Her eyes made one desperate appeal and then conceded to the reality of my malevolence. She must have realized that I had been planning revenge for a long time, preconceiving the moment in which I would leave her stripped of defences. All she wanted now was to make herself invisible. I could see that her most urgent need was to dematerialize. And for a split second I felt sorry that she should have to face public humiliation. Her past hadn't provided for this form of dramatic scene.

My cape was over my arm. I felt indomitably superior to everyone in the room. I could have resisted a line of stampeding elephants. I was scrupulous to the last detail in leaving nothing behind. My cigarette-case, my lighter, the book I was reading. I wasn't going to leave a trace of myself to the crowd. I felt I was standing at the entrance to a storm waiting for the thunder. Dry rain. Burning clouds. The train advancing through the sky would come later.

I peaked on the sustained momentum of my anger and clattered direct across the floor to the exit. The force with which I left tore Anaïs's face from her. I had the feeling that I had whisked away a movie strip. She would never again regain the same face. She would run after me begging me to return the characteristics which belonged to her eyes, her nose, her voluptuous mouth. But I was already outside the door, my head rocking in the cool air on the boulevard. Punishing Anaïs had been like metaphorically breaking Henry. I wanted to walk over them like dolls, leave their bodies holed by my spiked heels. I knew that without me as the strategic inclusion in Anaïs's triptych, her affair with Henry would collapse. It was her desire for me, her fascination with my looks that had her wish to confiscate my husband. In her mind it was the nearest she would get to me. She must have hoped that Henry's love-making would resemble the way he took me. By my action I hoped to break her sexual fantasy of possessing me through Henry. I wanted neither of them in my life.

I felt too indignant to return home immediately. I needed to go into shops and spend the money I didn't possess. I wanted to meet the perfect stranger and be driven in an open car to a château outside Paris. This man would have hired Edith Piaf to come and sing to me. The bedroom would be a forest of red roses. It would take him hours to find me curled up on a four-poster. When we touched, we would be metamorphosed into leopards.

I walked to keep pace with my anger. I went straight through the crowds without seeing individual faces. A red coat, a blue one, a black, nameless faces directed toward meeting-points in the city. I was in the process of shedding my past. A hard white light reached me down the avenues. I kept thinking that if I could sustain this power, if my nerves could endlessly compute this optimum chemistry, I would have the secret to life. I would never die. I wasn't in a hurry. I walked with unfaltering confidence. People who disappeared over my right and left shoulders must have assumed that I had an appointment. They couldn't have conceived that I was walking toward the realization of my future. There was no universal accompaniment of the nature of which Artaud spoke, no lions coming to meet me out of the autumn sun, no messenger leading me through the crowds by having me hold on to the stem of the gold flower he cupped in one hand. Instead, there was me and the unobstructed future. I felt liberated from the restrictions that had bound me no matter how tentatively to a domestic past. I wasn't needed. I hadn't been for a long time. I had viewed the web in which Henry and Anaïs had got trapped as a safety net, and the inextricable fascination I had developed about their sex lives had kept me back. If I was to live purposefully I had to form a life independent of their attraction to decadence. I had nothing to contribute to art. The belief I had in the novel I would eventually come to write was an affectation, a delusion I maintained to condone my life-style. Like so many others who lived dangerously, I believed that my experiences would be embodied through fiction. It was easier for Anaïs. As a psychological diarist she was able to convert living into art. I didn't want to be a part of the relentless analytic principle of writing. It wasn't me. Artaud had spoken of the black rainbow that springs from a poet's mouth. I wanted light. I had spent my years sucking on other people's shadows.

Drink had assuaged any other curiosity I possessed about my potential.

And now I was striking out toward a more realized dimension. All the chaotic possibilities that intrude on singular direction were being eliminated. There was just me and the clear air. An emptying out and a corresponding lucidity of thought.

And as I walked, losing my chemical high but not the resolution I had set myself, the figure of Artaud came into my mind. I wondered where he was at this moment. When he appeared, in and out of temporary adjustments in asylums, he was like someone come back from the dead. Black suited, irrefutably prophetic, he carried the air of an initiate into hermetic cults. I should have been afraid of his impassioned loathing of humanity, but I wasn't. He had broken chairs and glasses but had never once touched me. He understood my deepest needs as a woman seeking individuation and freedom from male tyranny. There were times when he looked up and the tragic affirmation of suffering in his eyes communicated with all the damaged, wounded beings who lived as outsiders. If Artaud had suddenly appeared on the other side of the street, I wouldn't have been surprised. He would have been moving through the crowds as someone set apart. Poor, dishevelled, but unmistakably a visionary.

But it was good to be walking with him in my mind. In this crucial time I needed the support of someone who would understand. Life around me was diverse, indifferent, uncaring of the individual. A builder on a low scaffolding whistled as I went by. A fruiterer was arranging his display of apples, plums, peaches, a woman in a pink Chanel jacket was standing face up to a fashion arrangement, her eyes taking in the line of a black cocktail skirt, and then travelling from mannequin to mannequin, and in the process evaluating how she would look in a dark-green jumper, a beige-coloured crochet skirt.

Everyone was preoccupied with their particular moment of consciousness. Artaud was mine. His image was walking parallel with me toward the river. In my mind he was waving his arms with declamatory gestures. Although he wasn't addressing me in person, he was glad of the presence I afforded. We were reassured by each other's company. I wanted to reach the quays and present myself to the water lights sliding along the river's spine. I needed that as the external mirror to my inner changes.

I slowed my pace. I had been walking like someone pursued, but now I let the afternoon drift with me. The air was cool and alerted high spots in my cheeks. I sat down at a table outside a café and let the blood rush slow. I was in a quiet quarter. I could hear children playing in a school yard. Their voices were timeless. They could have been the same ones I heard at school, lying in the dormitory upstairs, window open on the playground below. It was always same excited hum, as though one was hearing it in a dream. I had come this far. My bridge into the future was still an imaginary one, a trajectory pointing to the edge of the world. If it didn't quite reach, I might have to take off my shoes and wade the remaining distance to the shore. And would there be others? Artaud had spoken of such a place. I was starting to realize that everything is possible. The moonlight on that shore might form the perfect tent in which I could sleep. I was going to try for that place. Paris was rusty – the sun was a wounded lion in retreat. I would see Artaud somehow, somewhere before I left.

I got up again and headed for the river. The light on my face told me I had been found. I would go on searching forever.

Chapter 5

Sometimes there are holes in my thinking. I pursue a tangent and disappear along that trajectory only to find I've achieved a blank. I can't remember the train of thought that precipitated my inquiry. The disquiet I feel is similar to the depersonalized crisis that characterizes my coming out of coma after shock treatment. For a brief time there's no one there. I'm convinced that if I looked for myself in a mirror, the image wouldn't register. I am the idea of Artaud. He is absent.

I have to create a person. I am a legend to the few who germinate underground cults. If I were to die today, my readership would have been four hundred, my published output minimal – but my name, that's something else. A name is like a flag folded and put away for next year's carnival. Only, the flag increases in size and one day it spills orangely, mauvely, redly across the blue sky. Young people looking up to see the banner lolling on the air are alerted to an arrival, a happening.

I imagined that for myself, not that it alleviated my suffering. At best the conception lived as my way of outraging bourgeois standards. I care nothing for literature. Novels are invariably a social pretence, a way of confirming the rationale which informs an age. It's only in the novels of Jean Genet that I see the vulnerability and power of poetic vision attempting to transform life. Genet is so much in love with death that I swear he would kiss the fangs of a cobra. I can smell the bitter-sweet pain in his work. It has the scent of crevices in which ivy has rooted, it's like the perfume imprinted on a woman's scarf buried in her drawer. But Genet celebrates the erotic. I have transcended sex. My body is that of a black angel's. If Ferdière, and all the doctors who have certified me mad, could see my true identity, really see as a form of knowing, they would open the gates of the asylum to me. I would make for the acclamation that awaits me in Paris, the open car parting the crowds gathered to meet the chosen one. I am waiting. My endless letters to friends, acquaintances, assumed sympathizers, all state that my gift is dependent on my being free. More than that, I had discovered a universal language. I had retrieved the word from its burial in the garden at the centre of the world. I had fished it out of a gold box overgrown with ivy. Cabbalists, alchemists, ethnographers, anthropologists, semanticists, all had attempted through their various sciences to retrieve the metaphor that had incarnated consciousness. I had brought the secret with me to Rodez. If the other inmates knew, they would burn me in the garden. I have to use pencils with which to write my text, otherwise they overturn my ink-bottles and thumb blotches across my page. It is not I who am mad. It is they who incite in me the responses of a madman. Why else would I attempt to set fire to my room?

Unknown to Ferdière I am preparing to write the book which will put an end to all others. I have it in my head. When the time is right I shall break silence. I have already offered a preparatory book to the world. Unfortunately, the edition is lost. It was printed in a very limited edition, but disquiet on the part of government ministers, the Church and the police caused it to disappear. There is only one copy left, which I do not own but which is in the hands of one of my daughters, Catherine Chilé. She was a nurse in 1934 at the Hôpital Saint-Jacques, where she was training to be a doctor. She has been trying to reach me for years, but is prevented from doing so by demonic influences. I feel her near me all the time. She sits reading in a black cloak covered with stars. When she looks up, her front teeth are in the form of two As. She will be one of the daughters I take with me to paradise. We shall sit in a dark-blue pavilion and resume the universal story, the one in which the poet is the first-born letter of the alphabet and resonates for all time on the tongues of panthers, jaguars, leopards the exquisite lyricism of birds giving clear voice in a forest dawn.

Instead, I pitch my voice at the white walls of my cold room. When the doctors make their rounds I hide under the bed. I shall answer only as the voice of a concealed oracle. To know me is a revelation. I shan't have my light shine on the commonplace. Ideally, I'd like to walk into a dark forest, lie down with the deer and find a poem hidden under a wild strawberry leaf. At night, there would be other poets gathered round the fire – Baudelaire, Rimbaud, Lautréamont, Trakl. Nerval sketching out maps to an invisible blue mosque, Hölderlin holding the skull dug out of his grave and placing flowers in the cranial fissures. They would be joined together after their suffering. I would sit in that circle and be known.

My illness is that I wanted poetry to be truth. I hoped to live in the imaginative reality created by art. My work demands a physical response. In the same way as a patient receives a transplant, so my intention is to have the poem transferred to the reader or listener as an organic entity. My spiritual daughters were altered by my light. They saw and they heard.

Last night I had a vision. I receive them all the time, but this one was vividly immediate. I was walking on the outskirts of a city. There were waste lots, a man with his head in his hands sitting on a wooden box, the rusted chassis of a car dominating the foreground. It could have been cinema. There was a cracked house opposite. I was startled by the fact that the windows blinked

104

like eyes. Their co-ordination was human. I knew I had to make my way towards this house on the opposite side of the precinct. I began involuntarily to head direct towards the man seated with his back to me. He showed no curiosity at my approach, no quick swing of the head over one shoulder as a reflexive defence at being covered. As I narrowed on the man, I had the feeling that it was myself who was seated there. I knew in the split second before he turned round that it was my own face I would see. I was confronting my other. And in the instant I was confused. I didn't know if he was the true me or a double. For some reason I picked him up under the arms and began pulling him towards the opposite house. There was no weight involved in this. It was like carrying light dropped out of the sky. What was curious was that words kept pouring out of his pockets. Unformulated alphabetic clusters in blue, red, gold and violet littered the ground. It was like an inexhaustible child's alphabet, the chaos of letters sometimes taking on sense, but most often splitting into inchoate fragments. I wanted to stop and retrieve the trail of scintillating words, but I realized this would take a lifetime. They were travelling away from the man like the formations of a galaxy. Long splinter nebulae were branching from a spiral arm. At the centre of this formation was the word. I could sense that. I could feel the vibration connect direct with my central nervous system.

I moved towards the house, confused as to whether I was the captive thrown over a stranger's shoulder, or if it was I attempting to remove an impostor by burying him. I had lost the notion of identity. I was split by the duality I realized existed in all life. What I entered wasn't a door but a square mouth. I found myself on the iced-over surface of a purple tongue. The place was a mausoleum. There were corpses buried in ice-trays, stacked right and left under an arched ceiling. In my vision, I stayed there a long time waiting for oracular speech. I stood anticipating the message that would issue from the glottis. But there was only the profound silence of a burial vault. I had to take the risk. I carried my double to the entrance of the throat

tunnel. I positioned him there and listened to the dull reverberation transmitted by the abyss. It sounded as though a waterfall
was crashing into a hollow. I hesitated, then pushed him through
the constricted opening into the unknown. It wasn't murder so
much as rebirth. I had helped my double into the cycle of reincarnation. I hoped never to hear from him again. I wanted him
to be cosmically absorbed.

I left that burial place and came out into the white sunlight.
The landscape had changed. The car wasn't there, the billions
of words scattered across the ground had disappeared. I was in a
familiar quarter of Paris. I headed for a café and regained consciousness in my room at Rodez.

I tell you this because my life is composed of such visions.
There are those who all of their lives cross such cosmic spaces
on an inner map that they render the function of physical travel
obsolete. The dangers involved are those of mirage. The city
reached is an illusory one. The vine unloads diamond-shaped
grapes, a woman dressed in nothing but a transparent emerald
veil leads the arrival through hashish clouds to a silk bed that
floats on an underground lake. To stay there is to go mad, but
having once explored the visionary cities, it is impossible to return. Opium takes me to the places where I am most at peace.
I can float there. I am no longer subject to the ravaging mental
and physical pains I experience without drugs. Hallucination is
indispensable to my existence. I should like to breathe colour
out of my nostrils. I should like to walk down the corridor on
fire and confront Ferdière through flames incapable of melting
my skin.

Instead, I am deprived of an identity. I am told that the auth-
oritarian routines of hospital life are more important than ven-
turing down the road to the ruined château where the Marquis
de Sade looks up from whipping a line of Tahitian bottoms to
see an eagle suspended above him, the gift of a mountain rose
in its claws. I am informed that employment, tax returns, paying rent, establishing good relations with neighbours, setting up
a healthy bank account, are all more important to living than

making sustained contact with imaginary kingdoms. If images comprised material wealth, poets would be the richest beings on earth. Instead, by some inverse alchemical process, the image arrives in the world as debased currency. Poems no more help a poet than glass diamonds do a jeweller. Ferdière refuses to let me out poor. He speculates that I'll wander the streets and end up being arrested. Detained for vision. But my mission is a singular one: to liberate the imagination. For too long it has been sat on by governments. Banks and business corporates have attempted to bury it beneath concrete foundations, institutions have reduced it to a dead rationale, universities have repressed the marvellous and replaced it with social realism.

I want to search through the streets of Paris and find the house in which the imagination has taken refuge. It may be resident in the attic above a brothel, or be discovered in the unused bedroom in a carpenter's house. Its purpose is always to surprise. I may go up the stairs, open a door and encounter beauty and terror in one blinding flash. And perhaps sitting heaped up on purple flags I shall encounter the androgyne, green eyes and dark-blue hair, hands in the form of leopard's paws, his dream so intense that a forest of statues hangs in suspension from an eye-beam. Or shall I surprise an illuminated triangle, just a simple triangle transmitting the great chain of images, or a woman with a lake between her open legs, the archetypes viewed inside her vulva, their endless permutations taking place like the rise and fall of stars? My journey is to reclaim the state of deathlessness in which we dream reality rather than impose a social structure on consciousness. This isn't a mystical undertaking. I have so little respect for writing that I extinguish cigarettes on the page in which I have work in progress. My text is a voyage towards the imaginative source.

And Mexico? I travelled there. It was my one excursion outside Europe. I didn't go there to experience initiation into peyote rites or to recount a travel narrative, but to find a race of people who could follow me in my ideas. I went in search of the Tarahumara Indians. I wanted to excavate their mythologies, have

107

them resonate in my psyche. I was looking for an image of revolution that accorded with my own. The voyage out from Antwerp was interminable. I used the month-long crossing to detoxify. I had a small supply of opium with me, but I was determined not to use it. I needed alert senses to apprehend the new. If I took peyote I wanted to be clear in preparation for its effects. A sailor repeatedly tried to get under my blanket at night. I had to fight him off. He glowered in the dark, his body smelling of rum, semen and hemp. For a week I fought with this man before I threatened to curse him. I told him I would have the flesh fall off his bones in a month. He would neither eat nor drink. He would die in a state of wasting delirium. He believed it. I got out my wooden sword and he took fright. If I spared him, it was because I was busy with other things.

I rarely appeared on deck. I kept to my fetid cabin. I was in a state of fevered detoxification. I kept seeing the drowned rise from the ocean floor, fish-eaten skeletons swarming towards our boat, they mobbed through my hallucinated sleep. I would make up shivering despite the intense heat in the sleeping-quarters. I knew that if I appeared in this state I risked being put in a strait-jacket and arrested on arrival at the next port. I had a bottle of whisky in my trunk, and I used it to restore myself from muscular spasms which contracted my chest, stomach and legs. My intestines felt like burnt leather. I expected to die on the high seas. I no longer cared. The blue of the sea and sky formed an abstract cube. At night I would look out at the mineral stars, megatons of crystal receding into black space. I was slowly purging my chemistry, editing out one drug to receive another. Part of me hoped secretly to be united with peyote in a chemical marriage. Only then would I know the love that women had denied me. I would be poured across the galaxy in a state of ecstatic mental orgasm.

We finally put in at Cuba. I was already penniless and had to face travel in Mexico as a destitute. I had come here to look for a new idea of man. I found myself in a savage landscape of sun and stone, the faces of gods cut into the mountains like agonized petroglyphs. The baked air was charged with sacrificial rites. I had the feeling that at times I was travelling through the body of a flayed god.

I was also suffering acute withdrawal symptoms inside the god's contorted body. I had been taking seventy grammes of opium a day in France, and in the process of my journey overland towards the mountains of North Mexico I threw away my short supply of heroin. That little sachet of substance, intended for my veins, ended up in a parched river course. I remember being struck by the incongruity of things: the juxtaposition of heroin and the incandescent stone claw against which the sachet lay. Two things which should never have met were married under a sky catching along the edges like burning paper.

As we neared the Tarahumara village of Norogachic, we could hear thunder. I could feel the electricity shooting through my horse. The creature was unnerved; a drum was banging inside its head. Several times it shied, almost unsaddling me. Lightning zigzagged across the sky like a shot zebra. We were at an altitude of eighteen thousand feet. I was half dead. I felt the storm would precipitate a seizure. I was at that state of nervous strain when the vibratory motor of an insect sounds like the roar of a car entering a tunnel beneath a city. I needed drugs to kill the pain, but I couldn't suggest to my guide that we went back down the slopes to retrieve something I knew could never be found again. I had the vision that eagles would attack us. Their wing-beats would lift the dust around us into the air. They would carry us off. I would be lifted in hooked talons towards an eyrie on a mountain-ledge. Laid out on grass littered with the bones of prey, I would be slowly eaten. I saw myself reborn from an eagle's egg, my skin covered in feathers, my hands and feet given the form of claws.

The thunder was a prelude to my entry to the village. It was a sign of arrival, the initiatory clue for which I was looking. Once I fell off my horse, cut my arm on a stone, and had to be placed back in the saddle by my guide. A raindrop flashed like a tear across the back of my hand. But still the downpour wouldn't

109

come. Everything burnt to a red intensity. As we neared the first of a succession of villages, I could see diseased Indians struggling off mats, their bodies eaten by famine and illness, emaciated, searching for help from somewhere – the earth, the sky, the impossible demented person I must have appeared to them. What could they know of my own desperation? No heroin, opium, nothing but the chance of being initiated into a peyote rite, my brain on the point of exploding, the landscape unrelieved in its marking up portentous configurations: magic, sacrifice, sex. There were groups of Indians masturbating by the roadside. Cocks resembling the abundant cactus, they worked with fixed intensity on their totemic shafts. I was enraged. This sexual display was aimed at turning me back. It was an attempt at occult reversal. I was looking for a cultural revolution. I was faced by a people and landscape carved out of the sun. Red and red. I expected to see lions sitting in the clouds, flame standing on the mountain-tops.

The thunder had moved off. Not a drop of rain to cool my molten blood. I was in the wrong place. Mexico, Mexico had betrayed me. I was turning into a solar effigy. I was meat cooking for vultures. I had become this dislocated assemblage, this piece of damaged geology. And I would have to push my depleted organism higher up the mountain to find my tribal teachers. Already the rarefied air was dissociating my head from my body. I was losing all sense of reality. It was a long journey to reach my hands, and long-distance instructions had to be transmitted to have my feet obey. I had forgotten the civilization I had left behind, the one I had denounced so fiercely in my cultural talks in Mexico City. But I knew instinctively that I didn't belong to this blood-stained parcel of earth on the edge of the world. The roar in my head was that of the sun. I would be found as the blackened discharge of a volcano.

There were lines of Egyptian anserated crosses cut into stone. Spears, trefoils, acanthus leaves, petroglyphs in which mythic creatures faced each other in eternal combat. I felt I was being swallowed into a serpent's bowels. I was a month in travel to

110

reach the village where the peyote rite was still enacted, and twelve days in the village waiting for the ceremony. My paranoia was shocking. I expected to be murdered and kept to my hut. The Indians regard whites as beings abandoned by the spirit. I was an anomaly in an indigenously ritualistic tribe. I expected my skin to be flayed and hung on a pole. And again thunder without rain. It was like a drum being played behind the purple cloudline. Dry storms that exacerbated the body's electric impulses. I was beginning to think the climate was a product of my imagination, and that the thunder was inside my head and not above the mountains.

I was in a state of irredeemable despair. I realized the Indians were out of touch with their primitive rites. They would perform their dance rather than live it out ceremonially. My coming here was already tented by disillusionment. My mind had never felt so disconnected from the outer world. When the dances began, wood fires blazed on all sides towards the sky. Goats were sacrificed, their organs cut out and placed on a branchless tree-trunk. Ten mirrored crosses, representing the invisible masters of peyote, were established on the perimeter of the circle. The peyote had been distilled in a jar, and a hole was dug to receive the spit from our mouths. I was on the point of blacking out. This time the thunder really was in my head. I could see a black sun rising. Twice I collapsed and had to be pulled up by the dancers. Water was sprinkled over my head. I was laid on the ground at the foot of an enormous beam on which three sorcerers sat during the dances. I drank the peyote and, as the rite demanded, spat into the hole dug for this purpose.

We were preparing to kill the sun when it rose at the end of the night's rituals. There was blood as the sorcerers cut into their own flesh, and shrill, birdlike cries as they invoked the prophetic. What I remember in retrospect is the elimination of time that the drug induced. I no longer questioned the reason for my existence. I understood that I invented life rather than it me, and that I created my own imaginative cosmos, and that if I accepted this I should cease to have the blocks that came about through my questioning how inspiration is received. For three days, the happiest in my life, I was free of physical suffering and the relentless mental torment that seems to have been attached to me from birth. Far more so than heroin, peyote arrested my suffering. I was simply being. There was no pressure to do, no obligation to own to an identity that could be categorized by the social world.

I slipped in and out of visions for the duration of the drug. I saw myself lifted up to the sun. Lion-faced, gold, I was married to fire. I returned with a sun in my belly, an alchemical deposit that spread through my veins with the message of health and longevity. As long as I was in this drugged state, I feared nothing. Images appeared fluently and without threat, no matter if their content was minatory. My body began to lose temperature as I was earthed. My fall from visionary flight was a slow one. I was returning nerve impulse by impulse to the temporal. It was like waking from a dream by gradual, diminished impressions. I became conscious again of the interdependent faculties of my body – my hands, my feet, my respiration. I was shivering and in a state of dehydration. I realized I was clear of the experience, and also that I was uncured of the nervous dilemmas I had hoped peyote would eliminate. What I had known was an interlude in suffering. What I wanted was a cure.

I needed to get away from the Tarahumaras. I still feared I might die in a blood sacrifice and be crucified on poles outside the village. And I needed the drugs that kept me alive.

We made a journey back to Chihuahua, my depression growing as I realized that my vision of the primitive had failed me. There were incurably sick Indians in every village. Who was I to expect an immediate cure, with a body both culturally and genetically separated from these people? I was dejected and desperate for heroin. The landscape was ravaged. Visually it appeared like surrealism hallucinated. I thought I could see a black chain suspended from the sun, and, hanging from it upside-down, the body of Edgar Allan Poe.

My passage back to France was a dispiriting one. I sailed in a boat called *Mexico* direct to Saint-Nazaire. The long crossing increased the sense of disillusionment I felt with both the primitive and civilized worlds. I had been rejected by both. Neither offered me the realization of a vision I had come to recognize as shared by the very few who generation after generation carry that gift in their bare hands through the build-up of traffic, the manic depersonalization of business. But the few go underground carrying torches through the dark, faces smeared by war-paint and car oil, and appear much later transformed by light. They emerge from the tunnel as the representatives of a new century. Fame is the reconstitution of a broken life without the individual being present. And posterity is simply another injustice accorded the man who didn't want recognition anyway. I was still suffering withdrawal symptoms on the interminable crossing to France. Nothing but an abstract blue horizon. It wouldn't have surprised me if trees had grown on the skyline, or if a camel had crossed the water in search of a blue oasis. I was stoned on emptiness. I had nothing to take back to Paris but my incurable malaise. I had to return to the French people as the inveterate outsider I had become. A man rattling words in his throat like rhythmic castanets.

And when we docked in the mid-November cold and the train crawled on its way to Paris, I was once again aware of my social status as a person without money or prospects. What did Paris with its effete literary cliques care about the peyote rites of a little Indian tribe confined to the inaccessible foothills of a mountain range in North Mexico? I was poor and hungry. No one came forward to welcome me at the station gates. The cold day sat on my shoulders like a dead cat.

At first my thoughts were about travel and the attempt to find somewhere on earth where capitalism had not bruised the imaginative spontaneity of its people. Truth in Europe had become the unforced prerogative of children. By the age of ten or twelve they were instructed to let go their spontaneity, their unconscious autonomy, and to leave their dreams behind like kites abandoned in the branches of a high tree. They were told

113

not to step back into the magic cave. And the ones who resisted, who refused to be imaginatively dispossessed, were the poets, artists, musicians and constructive anarchists who were automatically marginalized by the collective. What I faced for my vision was new detoxification cures, poverty, a regenerated cycle of homelessness and confrontations with editors sold into commercial thinking. I took it upon myself again to deconstruct the system. But I was tired. My work had become derailed. I began to insult people in the street. I sat outside cafés, unable to pay for my drinks, and tore holes in the continuous stream of anonymous pedestrians. What were they to me? But I was something to them by reason of my voice and my shrill, declamatory invective. In their eyes I was drunk or mad. But I was Antonin Artaud: the chosen one. The man whose eyes punched holes through the sun.

I took up again with Cécile Schramme, the Belgian girl who had come into my life before the voyage to Mexico. It was at this time that I was given a cane which was said to have belonged to St Patrick. I used this stick in bed. I placed it between myself and Cécile, and it was a dividing mark that she wasn't permitted to cross. I believed totally in sexual abstemiousness. Never again would I lose my seed to a woman. I had cultivated immanent light. If I portioned it out, it could be used against me. Blood is the most potent of all occult constituents. And mine would be concocted, travestied, deposited in hospital freezers. It was my duty to teach Cécile the art of psychic orgasm or kundalini. But she concealed her desire, her dissimulation impaired our understanding. No woman ever imagines that the man she has to do with is different from the others, and therefore demands a correspondingly separate approach to love. Cécile was incapable of adjusting. She professed to note the individual characteristics of our love, those particulars that set it apart from other relationships, but the image she gave me of herself was unreal. She betrayed me by falling in love with the misconceived idea of Artaud and not the person. She let fall to her parents her belief that I was mad. The news was out that

114

Artaud was insane, or that he was an emasculated pervert who used a cane instead of a penis to enter a woman. My name was vilified. It went around infested with flies. It became contaminated like rusty water trickling from a discontinued source. Old women in cafés laughed at me. Policemen scrutinized me. Cécile's parents wrote me a letter in which they said they were scandalized by my behaviour. Word had reached them that, during my abandoned Brussels lecture, I had spoken on the effects of masturbation on closed orders. I was caught up in an emotional holocaust. Cécile had already started to buy her trousseau. I set fire to the garments in the garden of the house in which she was living. White and ivory silk crumpled into black tatty smoke. This time it was a death rite. Whatever of my past belonged to France went skyward in a charcoal spiral.

It was then I decided to disown my name. Nothing but opprobrium had been heaped on the person of Artaud. Nails had been driven into my books and black roses heaped on my coffin. I had been left behind by the war which raged in my body. A few depleted cells remained as casualties. The action had moved on without me. Literary reputations were being made, films shot and theatre productions staged, and I was placed a thousand miles back down the road, thumbing for non-existent cars, all traffic dead on a Sunday morning in August.

And was madness a way out of the crisis or a condition I inherited at birth? I was too exhausted to sleep. I dreamt of sitting at the bottom of a dry well, away from the world, and spending my days in the company of toads. I would live on bluebottles, mosquitoes and crane-flies. My skin would become the green and brown of a toad's. My metamorphosis would be complete.

But always the practical call back to a reality I would have disowned asserted itself with terrifying rapacity. I should have liked to wake up to a world altered by the imagination, changed in the manner of a film projected on to a blank screen. What would the autocrat, the bureaucrat or the banker do faced with an alternative reality? How would they function in cyberspace?

The ministry of defence employee would look up to see a sky divided into three distinct colours: yellow, green and red. On each of the perfectly divided bands people would be sitting looking down at the world. In place of his familiar car the man would find an iguana basking in the warmth. Exotically coloured sea shells would litter streets now overrun by ginkgo trees. And then the repetitive demands of the material world would have disappeared. Why is it we don't tire quicker of seeing the same environmental props and the same undifferentiated physical characteristics in our species? We go on receiving sterile information because we accept it as insignificant in comparison with our imaginative action.

I used to sit and meditate on these things. In the raw winter following my return to Paris, I was so cold and hungry that I begged in the streets. My work had reduced me to the ultimate social ignominy – vagrancy. Wrapped in a holed blanket, my fingers shaking from exhaustion and drug need, I hung out in the streets of Montparnasse. And people weren't generous. When I received money it was usually from the poor. I was emaciated. I hid in alleys and doorways when I saw the police on their routine patrols. I had a dread of being thrown inside. Social misfits are drugged and walled up in asylums.

It was on one of those afternoons when I strayed across the city that I met a woman whom I thought I knew. It was the American, June Miller. I had dreamt her into being the previous night. She still had a luminous dream-light framing her face, as though she hadn't broken free of the oneiric chrysalis. I knew her instantly. I had created her. We spoke to each other like two people who had spent their lives inhabiting one another's dreams. Together we must have known so many places; we must have surprised ourselves inside the burial chamber of a pyramid, on the roofs of high-rise buildings, on the backs of gazelles speeding across grasslands, walking on the moon, laying out a garden on the sea-floor. There was no end to the imaginative possibilities. What seemed certain was that we had exchanged one reality for another. Our meeting was no propitious intersection, it was a direct revelation. It occurred at a time when I had frozen my sexual impulse. Opium and heroin kill desire. I had entered into a state of unmediated androgyny. I could feel myself living on the dividing line between the sexes. In spiritual terms, I was complete.

But this woman was beautiful. She was sensual in ways that pronounced her femininity, and she was deeply unhappy. She had been out walking like me, in the hope of resolving inner dilemmas. She had made herself up to look provocative, but the effects on me were negative. I was able to be with her without expressing desire. I had trained myself to cut out instinctive needs, and to redirect the nerve messages inwardly. In that way I wanted nothing from life. June did, however. She was searching for a directional clue to her future. She imagined it would come about in the form of a new relationship, or by way of discovering something within herself that would extinguish the past. But neither event happened. In her desperation she had taken to patrolling bad quarters of the city. She wanted to bring out in others what she couldn't find in herself: the desire for promiscuity.

Our engagements were secret, and it appealed to my hermetic belief to meet her behind closed curtains, and to sit out the Paris afternoon or night in deep conversation. And because our meeting had come about through a dream, I continued to think of her as unreal. I was often situated in the context of a drug, so that my spoken findings acted independent of the conversation, or else I was so far isolated by nervous illness that my inner dialogue was obsessive. We communicated by sympathetic tangents. Our relationship was possessive. While we lacked physical contact, we were united on a deeper level. I could see myself looking out of her eyes; a face in each pupil. At that moment I had achieved the ultimate in renunciation. I was hers, and at the same time I was prostrate before my psyche, an initiate watching images form in an oval mirror. I said her to her once, 'I no longer know what is normal or supranormal. I know what is. That is all.' And it was like that. Our time together was one of mutual self-realization. It was a preparation for death, the

117

acceptance that who we are, rather than what we do, is the qualitative measure of truth.

It was a time in my life when nothing was happening creatively. I worked inside my head. My body became the materials for my work. I felt radically cut off from what was happening in the arts, and was too distracted to contest the mediocrity that was rapidly and oppressively attempting to cover Breton's trail. I lived by the strength of my inner dream. And, of course, I burnt. I had the power to burn as no one else on earth. Out of my volcanic rage kings were born. Men who went off to the spiritual deserts to reclaim their supremacy. I was mentally incarnating the great. My concepts were realities. All my inner ones were preparing for the apocalypse. I took lessons in interpreting the tarot pack. I was prepared actively to participate in the final revolution, the one that would make the protest of students, workers and political activists appear socially absurd. I could feel the imaginative dream building. I was like the nuclear physicist who realizes that fission can destroy the universe. Only my means would bring about a restoration of truth, a regeneracy of the unfissured dream, whereas science would torch the planet and leave it revert to the instinct of primordial survival.

By distinct degrees I began to acquaint June with my doctrine of the inner ones. I wanted her to begin her migration away from the world. She could become the alchemical woman surrealized by light, the one who mounts a staircase formed of blue slabs cut from the sky and goes all the way up to the top. My sisters of the heart would join her there. The view beyond was one of castles grouped around a lake. Those who participated in the grand design swam across that lake on the backs of purple fish. Our bodies would turn gold in the process.

But June wasn't easily shifted. She was too conscious of her presence as an attractive woman. The world noticed her. She needed that attention in the same way as I was dependent on drugs. She liked the fact that men admired her face, the curve of her figure, the length and shape of her legs. It was a part of her, and she both consciously and unconsciously cultivated such attention. But she was extraordinarily aware of inner events. She never tried to discredit my vision of Paris in flames. Sometimes I told her the exact time and place in which the holocaust would begin. A black magician would appear on the roof of a building overlooking the Cimetière Montmartre and point a blue finger at the sky. Then the flames would spread. Cataclysms would underpin the city. Cars would drive into the abyss. The police would open fire in the face of red dragons. June couldn't go this far, she couldn't connect with universal destruction. It threatened her sense of individuality. She would rather have seen the world changed by ideas – That old perpetuated belief that we can change ourselves and the world. Eventually I shouted: EVERYTHING MUST GO. YOU WILL NOT EVEN RECOGNIZE YOURSELF IN THE FIRE. I tore my clothes and my hair, I shriekingly declaimed my convictions. And she took no offence. She knew me for who I am. Others had thrown me out on the street, called the police, urgently summoned a doctor to stick a needle in my arm.

I have never found anyone who felt as I did. It's the reason for my deep loneliness. I search the streets constantly for the special one who will know me. June knew me in her own way, and in my lucid periods I accepted her limitations. She could never advance beyond the wall established by her own thinking. She came up against her own image and retreated in safety. I couldn't wrap a towel round her hand and command her to smash the mirror. I had demanded that of everyone. They had run back to the crowd with bleeding hands, proclaiming my madness.

A city alters when you come at it from a tangent of starvation. If I have eaten rats before being confined at Rodez, then I have also tasted the flesh on my hands from hunger. The Paris in which I starved and was shown the door by its literary editors was to me a city I knew only by night. I came to know the other Paris, the one inhabited by those who are too humiliated by poverty or illness to risk walking the streets by day. At first I had used the element of shock, the confrontational tactic to shame acquaintances into giving me money. But then I withdrew. I wrote *Les nouvelles révélations de l'être,* a prophetic work filled with numerical calculations and tarot interpretations. In it I told of my separation from the world. I wrote: 'I am not dead. But I am separated.' I had decided to reject reality. I received a vision at dawn. A red star became visible over Paris. It was too large: it was like the moon, only I saw it as radial, and each time I looked up its volume had increased and it was travelling at great speed towards our earth. I welcomed the sign. The whole sky was turning red. The planet was an avenging one. It represented the fire for which I had been waiting. At some point that blinding trajectory cut out, but I knew it would return. My whole body was vibrating with interstellar energy. I was the recognized one, the poet who anticipated cosmic catastrophe.

And June? I told her of my vision. She received it with her usual dispassionate sympathy. She was wearing a turban, a tight green skirt and matching shoes. Her lips left a dark-red stain on the rim of her tumbler. I wanted her to come with me to Ireland so that she would be with me in a sympathetic environment when the revelation occurred. But there was a distance in how she received me. The previous week, on one of my rare appearances in Paris by day, Anaïs had seen me standing outside Le Dôme, brandishing my Mexican cane and shouting out my immediate visions. June's interest in me had been visibly decreasing. And now I sensed in her a subtle change towards viewing me as mad. There was an unspoken judgemental value in how she observed me. I felt out of harmony with the vibration. My hypersensitivity allows me to watch a thought take shape in a mind. I see how it spirals into untruth or proceeds direct to communicate its content. June's thoughts were twisting into complex involutions. And I wouldn't stand for this.

I left abruptly, half expecting her voice to call after me down the stairs and to hear the sound of her heels in pursuit. But there was only silence. I stayed a moment before opening the door into the street, my rage consuming reason. In my mind I planned to come back after dark and paint the word WHORE on the entrance door to her building. I knew then that I had to leave Paris. June would rather root herself in the material ethos than join hands with me in the flames that would constitute the beginnings of a new world.

I got to Ireland on money borrowed from friends. I would never have to pay back my debts, as the capitalist epoch was at an end. I chose the island of Inishmore in the Aran Islands as a suitable location for my preparation to meet inhabitants from the red star. It was September. The time was near. I was in search of metaphysical heroes. The seasonal change, characterized by reddening bracken and the splash of yellow leaves, was to be reflected in the imminent planetary holocaust. I was a thin, drugged individual holding my hand up to the cosmos. I expected to receive a rose in my open mouth.

When I travelled over to Dublin I was destitute. I was afraid of dying before the end. I was told that I had been offensive in the street. I wanted to get into a monastery to find help, but the walls resisted my force. I found myself being physically constrained, metal biting into my wrists. It was the police, who were pulling me in a direction contrary to the one in which I intended to go. And the rest has become a part of my story. I was thrown into a cell, and six days later assigned a cabin on board the *Washington* sailing for Le Havre.

It was in the middle of the night that the steward and a mechanic came into my cabin carrying metal implements. The ferocity of my attack was such that I was placed in a straitjacket and handed over to the French authorities in Le Havre. I was led through the streets like a bear in chains. It was the poetic imagination that was on a trial. I had been physically prevented from serving as the visionary instigator of a new mode of consciousness. I, who had intended talking to dolphins and swimming on the back of a purple fish through underwater palaces, or cutting words constellated with minerals from the mountainside, was now reduced to the condition of a catatonic inmate. I had expected to see my visions crystallize as reality. I had thought a bird would tuck me under its wing and fly above

121

a whole tropical forest with me. Women would look up from trees to see me trailing a rainbow. When I spoke, my sentences would be visible in the sky. I had hoped for so much, and I was offered so little.

There are facts, and there are truths that live inside the factual which I can share with no one. Most of the essence of living goes with one into death. It is there like the nucleus of a DNA spiral. But madness is a constant way of presenting the interior. I wore my work on the surface of my skin like an indigo tattoo. Never again would I be silent about my particular vision of the world. I would attack reality like an airbrush artist gunning loud colour across a buried photograph. I would slash vicious tears in the fabric.

I wanted to break through to the other side. I had only to touch words and they went off like lit petroleum. Rodez was both the mollusc's shell in which I suffered and the stage on which I presented the various steps of my madness. The red curtain looked like a lion had fought it to shredded tatters. And no matter my exclusion from society, I staged my inner projects with the idea of the world as audience. I wanted to impale bourgeois literature on a dog's penis. To live is to survive oneself. I was travelling despite my isolation. The speed of thought had eaten up twenty or thirty lives. I was headed for a future in which I wouldn't be there to participate. Absence. It's the story of my life. The man in black who can't be seen for the black backdrop. I was preparing my own cathartic end. No eagles or a purple cloth thrown over the coffin – just a man projecting himself against the wall of his own mortality.

Chapter 6

Denise. For a long time I wanted to disown my name. After my experiences at Rodez, and my subsequent periods of treatment in a number of clinics, I had little inclination to historicize my past. My name was attached to specific terms of diagnosis. Ferdière's blue manila folder contained the biography of my madness. I could see my name marked up in black capitals: **Denise X**. The latter was all I would own to as a surname. It distinguished me. It was like wearing dark glasses inside.

What I resented at Rodez was the lack of sustained privacy. Even if I put my chair up against the door, someone would intrude – a doctor or an inmate carrying a paper dart in his mouth the way a cat runs with a bird. My methods of dress have always been highly individual, stylized and expensive in taste. When my father, who was a virologist attached to a team researching sexually transmitted diseases, crashed his Citroën on the night road, I was left as heir to his private fortune. He had divorced my mother soon after my birth. I was Denise, and he was my potential lover. In my childhood fantasy I was a white moon and he was a red sun. He would bite a chunk out of my side if he decided to leap. As a girl, I used to pick red camellias from the garden and place them in my hair. When Father was out, I used to make up precociously. I took my image from screen stars, singers, a world in which women highlighted their individual characteristics and accentuated a way of having clothes stand out. I used to buy these things clandestinely with money I stole from the maid. When I had enough, I would go and make a purchase in one of the second-hand theatre shops. I brought home a black boa, a red sequinned skirt, silk stockings with seams, and a pair of black satin gloves. These were my right to a separate identity, the Denise Father didn't know about. She was a secret between me and the mirror.

I would get so excited dressing up that the act became a sexual experience. I would become moist from realizing the extent of my provocativeness. I imagined I was dressing for a man and anticipating his excitement at watching me walk my second skin across the floor. Lacking a microphone I sang along to my kind of music: Bessie Smith, Libby Holman, Billie Holiday. I placed a pink camellia in my hair instead of a white gardenia. I was a torch singer about to live out my psychodramas on-stage. My raised eyebrows and dark lipstick were the external mask to my inner torment. I imagined the pianist sitting at a Steinway, a bowl of red roses on the top. Each time I breathed, the audience would shiver. I would take off one glove and then a second, my hands dramatizing the loneliness of my gestures. Love in the face of a rival. Age as it disfigures the actress. The woman in a pink velvet jacket who was once a man. I had my repertory. I prolonged my sessions for hours.

I was in such a state of high adrenalin that I found it difficult to reconnect and go back to being the undistinguished schoolgirl, Denise. I was disappointed in her. My schizoid faculties were coming more and more to identify with my histrionic persona.

In my imagination I was chauffeur-driven across Europe in a cobalt Daimler; the crowds waited for me outside concert halls.

My arms were too loaded with roses to carry another stem. Posters of me, cigarette in hand, face-net ambiguously veiling my features, my eyes like two sooty daisies of mascara, were posted all over foreign towns. In one of them I was promoted just on the shape of my legs, in another by the pencilled outline of my lips. My mystique fascinated my cult. My tastes in everything were published: cocktails, clothes, conjectured sexual preferences, music, food, shoes, books, theatre. I was under the scrutiny of a micrological public. If I made a gesture it was interpreted with analytic scrutiny.

I got to know my parts. I became more adept at switching roles. I could soon do so within minutes of Father leaving the house. What had taken me hours, was now an immediate accomplishment. I was the other.

And this was my undoing. I began to take risks, the daring of which considered objectively courted a recklessness that had to end in disaster. Adopting the compromise of a half-identity, I appeared at dinner in my school uniform but carrying a decorative evening bag and wearing under my skirt a matching G-string. My clandestine allusions to a double life appeared to be wasted on my father. I wanted to shock him, but he resisted all notice of the anomalies in my dress. He decanted half a bottle of whisky into his system after dinner, froze into his own blurred inner vision, and was lost to any sense of mutual dialogue.

But eventually it happened. I was overconfident. I got caught. I heard Father take the car out of the drive in the early evening. He was expected at a friend's house for dinner. The combination of heavy foliage and an indigo sky encouraged me in my mood of fantasy. I went into his bedroom, slipped out of my clothes, and with a light-fingered fever riffled through the drawers in which my mother had kept her lingerie. I expected my father to have kept items. And there they were. I was intoxicated by the tactile sensuality of each individual garment. I abandoned caution. I stood in front of the mirror dressed in a pair of red chiffon panties with a matching bra. I draped a pair of stockings over one arm, and posed. I gashed my mouth with a red lipstick. I was the scarlet woman.

I didn't have time to hear the door, and he was just standing there, eyes dilated to black bugs sticking on my body, patrolling the erogenous zones with electric intent. My mouth froze into an oval rictus. I was expecting a voice to explode across the silence, but there was nothing to break the intensification of a moment that expanded to a century there in the looking, before his urgent hands picked me up under the knees and bottom and positioned me on the bed. His hands were straining at his fly.

I had never heard anyone breathe like this. The rapidity was that of someone running up a steep flight of stairs. I had never held a man's body and the weight of muscle surprised me. I could never have known Father felt like this, his vertical hardness periscoping to find my place, adjusting the angle of entry and forcing with violent motion from his hips. When he was in, the immediate pain bit me, but then I settled to the undulating rhythm, the imposed control of a man both excited and terrified by his actions. I could sense this duality. He was excited by his own constraint. He was looking to convict himself of incest in the act of doing it. I continued with my spontaneous precocity. I lifted my legs high and folded them round his spine. It didn't take him long to reach his climax. And as soon as he had come he withdrew, manoeuvred off the bed and left the room.

In the course of the months to follow we went through the same unvoiced actions like a piece of theatre. I was compelled to repeat the process of dressing in my mother's lingerie and heels, sometimes slinging my school satchel over my shoulder as an additionally inciting accoutrement. I came to miss his approaches if he didn't come home unexpectedly and find me in a state of provocative undress. Instinct taught me to go further and further. I made my face up heavily. I dyed my pubic hair turquoise: I depilated myself and outlined the lips with rouge.

When it all ended, when Father gave up the game I had rehearsed with such aptitude, I began to suffer black-outs and violent mood swings. Not that it was that clear-cut: cause and effect rarely exist as an unmodified impulse, but rather as a quirky, tenuous possibility. Ferdière kept insisting I looked for experience that predated the recognizable trauma. Had it begun earlier? Did I fantasize incest? Was there an old man on the summer road, under the poplars, when I came home from school? Early, late. Ferdière pressed me back into the dark thicket. I could smell ivy, leaf rot. There was a grass snake in the ditch, an emerald lizard sunning on a stone, and deep in the wood a hut. Someone lived in there. They said it was a gipsy who dressed in rags and had leaves in his beard. When he lit fires, the bitter scent of blue smoke stained the air. There was a fox hanging on his door, its red brush suspending the animal's weight. Did he ask me inside, cajole me into submission? Did I feel him on me rough as the fox he had impaled on the door?

The summers were so long. I sat in them like someone at the bottom of a deep lake. Reality had vanished. It didn't exist in that timeless vacuum. But the leaves did. They coloured the afternoon green. Ferdière told me to go further. He didn't object to my sitting on his lap. It gave me a sense of being the seductress, the other me sheathed in pink sequins, my hair falling across my tear-dropping eyes. And I couldn't always find the way back or part the leaves to see the tiger's face staring at me.

Ferdière considered my delusions came from a compulsion to repeat the initial trauma. He thought my energies were directed into maintaining a cycle of perversion and restitution. Was my father a fixated paedophile? He wanted to know. Had he been starved of loving affirmation by my mother? Did he extend his sexual interests to molesting other prepubescent children?

I had to discover Father through Dr Ferdière. He took me on journeys to places I hadn't visited. He used to say poetry serves the same function, one of displacement. The reader finds himself in a landscape, physical or mental, created by the poet. It wasn't there before the images built it. He told me about Artaud, a poet who was also living at Rodez, and who had been experi-

encing great difficulties in establishing a division between imagination and reality. Ferdière placed great emphasis on the need
to imagine, the importance of transforming the material world
in the process of creativity, but he was equally aware of the
dangers entailed by this function. He wanted me to meet Artaud.
He told me a little about him. How he had published some
poetry and essays, and how he had been a member of the surrealist movement. He described Artaud's condition in non-clinical
terms. He told me his violent rages alternated with periods of
lucid calm when he questioned the rights of the authorities to
detain him in confinement.

This was the man I had passed in the corridor, a cigarette
twisted into his mouth, ink-blotches blued across his hands, his
baggy black suit falling off his emaciated body. I recognized
immediately that I shared no affinities with someone so crumpled into an innately volcanic rage. In addition he spat, but
deliberately, as though he was aiming at an invisible presence. I
had seen him shrieking, his declarative voice addressing a double,
an enemy, a doctor? I was frightened he would attack. He was
like a wild animal about to leap on a patient or orderly. So
when Ferdière suggested I became a friend to Artaud, I was shaken.
Every instinct advised me to avoid this man. His ferocity stormed
the walls of his room. He was forever beating on a surface, a
drum, a sheet of metal, something that afforded a percussive
rhythm with his screams.

When I first visited him he was in a quiet mood. I had come
from one of my more reassuring sessions with Ferdière; he had
provided the paternal figure I needed for the duration of our
meeting. We had backtracked into places in the psyche where
the beasts were tamer. Father wasn't there with flames coming
out of his penis. Mother wasn't there smiling for having abandoned me, her mouth telling me she would do it all over again.
'I regret nothing,' she had written to me as a child.

Artaud was sitting on his bed smoking. He was distracted by
inner preoccupations. His hair was a mess; he had cigarette-
burns on his nether lip as well as on his clothes. He didn't say

anything when I entered. He just went on looking at whatever it was which occupied his mind. He extended a gesture towards the one chair in the bare room, motioning me to sit down. Without taking the cigarette from his mouth, he said to me, 'The spell has been taken off me for an hour. They want to silence my occult knowledge. Paris will be on fire tomorrow. The city will disappear into the void.'

He levelled his black eyes with ferocity, and jolted back into the taut aftermath of his words. He looked like someone who was in such intense pain that any final system of events would be a preferable exchange for the agony of his inner vision.

'Fuck it,' he ejaculated, 'I've been an opium addict for twenty-five years. It was first prescribed for me when I was very young, when I had meningitis, and subsequently for neuralgic pains in the head. And here they won't give it to me. You understand, you must get me opium or heroin. Without it I can't function. People are put in asylums because they can't purchase sufficient for their need.'

I was alerted to the immediacy with which he engaged me in a conspirational conversation. He presupposed that I and the world were familiar with his condition. He had conceived of the fixed idea that he was being detained because of his occult knowledge. Let back in the world, he would manifest his true identity – that of the chosen one. He was also Heliogabalus. He told me how the latter had delighted in wearing women's clothes, and how he had covered his body in jewels, pearls, feathers, coral and luxurious oils. Wherever he travelled, the rites of debauch had to be performed outside a city. Three lines of men engaged in sodomy had to be presented outside the city. Three hundred bulls drew the giant stone phallus which had become the emperor's talisman. High as the Empire State Building, the thing had to be erected within view of the villa at which Heliogabalus was staying. He subverted the Latin world; he urinated in the temples and engaged in coprophilia with rent-boys in his empty marriage bed, the heaped imperial cushions embroidered with scenes from the priapic rites.

129

Artaud, too, wanted a purple jacket liberally blazing with jewels. He couldn't understand why the nation hadn't recognized the hieratic significance of his role as the leader of a new species. I noticed how he killed a cigarette on the back of a book, this act of disrespect being executed with a suitably pronounced contempt. There was an absolute purity somewhere at the centre of his emotive hurricane. He voiced his hatred of commercialism, opening it up like a fishmonger pointing a knife across a compacted seam. He wanted to make people aware that they were dying. He saw the error of Western capitalism as being a denial of death, a refusal to accept mortality as the end of personal assets. He advocated a conscious acceptance of death as an antidote to ego. Men should measure their success against the prospect of infinite impermanence, was what he kept repeating as a form of internal credo. It should register in consciousness the way a thermometer records temperature, was another of his declared beliefs. He saw life as inextricable from death. You could live only when you had accepted the interdependence of the two states. On this, he was absolutely clear. Hearing him talk about death was like watching champagne tick in a crystal glass.

I had reason to be frightened of this fulminatory man. He repeatedly punctuated the drift of his thought with jungle screams. He suggested that I had died and was now inhabited by a demon. He attributed states of alienation to possession. He and I and the other inmates were very probably simulacra. He kept returning to the notion that he had died and was now inhabited by Heliogabalus. He told me how the emperor liked to invite diseased people to his table and risk infection by the plague. One of his perversions was to go to bed with terminally ill people. He was also, according to Artaud, the most extravagant of gourmands, often beginning a meal at dawn which was to end at sunset.

Artaud praised Heliogabalus's idea of introducing space into the digestion of his food, and savouring dishes over a time when the sun passed through the four cardinal points. He was good on the body and obsessed with the idea of the psychic being reflected in the somatic. He told me of how he had walked the streets of Paris in a long white shirt to remind people that he had died. He had stood outside Le Dôme like that and been moved on by the police. He saw most world events in terms of their being directed against him. He told me from memory of the communication he had sent Hitler: 'In memory of the Romanische café in Berlin one afternoon in May 1932, and because I pray God give you the grace to remember all the wonders by which he has gratified your heart this day.' Artaud wanted me to remember this. He claimed that the Führer had inhabited his body for six months and that he knew of his work. Hitler had wanted to siphon occult configurations from his mind.

I was uncomfortable. I didn't want to be drawn into this chaotic vortex in which despots goose stepped across the stage. Artaud was screwing himself up like someone attempting to contract to a prickly ball – a hedgehog poking its defensive spines at the inquisitive fox. He was telling me that in the Les Deux Magots, Le Dôme, La Coupole, and all over Paris, people were plotting personally to destroy him. The resulting electricity was aimed as shock waves at his brain. He was certain they knew the exact measurements and weight of his mind. He told me that the number of his brain cells corresponded exactly to the two million fibres which had made up the cane he had taken with him to Ireland. That cane, so he believed, would rematerialize on his release from the asylum. It would drop slowly out of the sky as a sign of his spiritual mission.

I shifted nervously. Flashbacks of my father, all concentrated lust and mellow cologne, bringing his face up so close to mine that it was featureless, were invading my head. Unresolved stuff, lifting like dust off the road as the mistral arrives, was coming back at me after my session with Ferdière. There was always this delay, the images clustering into the aftermath of our probe. I was beginning to feel I couldn't cope with this double madness. Artaud was using his knee as an ashtray. He was cutting counter-thematically across his narrative with bizarre tales about peyote and priests who danced themselves to a state of prophetic frenzy. He told me we had all to go out and form a huge circle in the asylum grounds. When we had done so, a snake would appear and lick our faces individually. That saliva would have us revert to children. We would be saved. We would see the world re-created.

His vision oscillated between the obscene and the innocent. When his eyes looked up, as though entreating a way out of suffering, one expected them to colour with the sky. But when they narrowed with a directed animosity, they were charged with a corrosive hatred. Artaud was being eaten by his own acids.

Without warning, he took up a heavy stick and began beating a percussive rhythm on a large block of wood which he employed as an improvised drum. He accompanied himself with discordant shrieks, ululating bird or monkey whistles, his dementia slapping the walls. I couldn't take any more and was frightened he would attack me. He was pitched into what Ferdière had called his own idea of breath, and the language he had invented to describe his inner pain. I hurried out of the room, his screams pursuing me down the corridor. I found security with a number of patients who were sitting reading in an uninviting blue room. I knew then that I had to get away from Rodez. My compulsive fantasies were as much a symptom of the present as a motivation from the past.

And over the weeks I avoided the hysterical man who called himself a poet. My refusal to meet him was construed on his part as complicity in the general occult pact to destroy him. He sent me letters saying that he knew a car was coming for me late at night to take me to Paris, where I was consorting with infamous magicians who met in a café almost directly across from the Taverne Labrunie. He was convinced that I was making regular visits to the capital to engage in practices that would lead to his dissolution. He had seen me run across the lawn in a red coat while a car waited for me outside the gates. Two hooded men were seated in the front, the masked figure who got into the back with me being a member of the government who would subsequently defect to the Nazis.

132

His letters, his accusations were written with an extraordinary concern for detail. The factitious gave an air of credibility to his derangement. I dreaded his communications. Executed in different coloured inks, slashed and burnt, the twisted artefact menaced by way of its implicit threat. After reading the first two or three. I left them untouched, but they generated hysteria in me, and I had a nurse remove them from my room. I didn't want to make the least contact with his needling curses, his bold lettering illustrated with hermetic symbols, prophetic declarations.

Eventually Ferdière put a stop to Artaud's letters. And these, for all the anger Artaud directed at psychiatrists, showed an unusual respect for Ferdière. Or was he frightened of being transferred from the reasonably enlightened ethos at Rodez to the sort of brutal asylum treatment he had already experienced? It wasn't deference he showed Ferdière, it was more a form of intellectual consideration. Artaud's monomania tended to exclude the possibility of intellectual companionship. He had broken with everyone, and ended up as tyrannical wreckage in madhouses, where his genius was hardly to be differentiated from the ravings of other patients. This was his problem. He needed someone as discerning as Ferdière in order to be realized as an individual.

Everyone inside believes in their own system of the universe. We are all planetary inhabitants of our imbalanced microcosm. Now that I can see my illness for what it was, I can understand the solitary vision of the psychotic, and the attention that pathological symptoms acquire. In my own case I see that madness is a compensation for the singer I had failed to become. Unable to live out my fantasies under the spotlights, to pick up one red carnation from the hundreds thrown on-stage and place it in my hair as a gesture of glamour, I entered into an inner world that in turn demanded notice from the outer one. My imaginative trajectory proved unassimilatable with reality. I was the crazy woman lifting her skirts at dinner parties, going out in the streets in cabaret clothes, sequinned dresses in the mid-afternoon, and singing in department stores, outside cafés, wherever I was sure to have a surprised audience. I knew that Edith Piaf had begun as a girl singing in the streets and I wanted to follow her. If I couldn't be a singer, I wanted to be an actress. And when I began sexually experimenting with men, I found none of them were as good as my father. It was the ritual I missed. My undressing, and posing before the mirror in bra and panties, waiting for the apprehensive rush of my father, who had been watching as a surreptitious voyeur for a long time, before catching me as if by surprise. I couldn't find a man or a woman willing to participate in this game of suspense. The men whom I took as lovers were too fast. They didn't smell of Father's cologne. They were brutally impulsive and dominated by the need for self-gratification.

If I took gay men back with me, they would allow me to dress them up in jewellery and silk lingerie, mascara and any number of couturier hats. This afforded me pleasure. I would pay them to submit to the dictates of my fantasy. Made up luxuriously in drag, stilted on spike heels, hands on hips, I would have my hybrid pasha walk round and round the room, while I masturbated. I had heard of men doing this, paying female prostitutes to adopt various provocative costumes, but never of women acting out this predominantly masculine role. I fingered myself ostentatiously, and sometimes drew a whip across a bottom.

My needs became progressively more extreme. I had developed into a perverse nymphomaniac, but one whose desire was not easily satisfied. I began spending my fortune recklessly. I recruited men from gay clubs, and when I grew bored with drag queens, I enlisted women. I wanted them to pretend they were me waiting for Father. They had to dress in my clothes, they had to prepare themselves with agonizing attention to detail in the mirror I had used to attract Father. If one managed to empathize sufficiently with my own propensities, I would take her as a man. My nights were spent in endlessly trying to recreate the insatiable appetite Father had given me. No one would ever again find the sensory spots, or communicate the nerve hits that Father had given me. He was my complete lover.

I had to communicate a lot of this to Ferdière. My breakdown was also characterized by acute symptoms of nervous exhaustion. I was often too weak to get out of bed, and at such times I was terrified that Artaud would get into my room. Ferdière considered and advised. Incest wasn't a new study with him. Systematic, conscientious inflictions of sexual abuse, as he called it, were acts in which the father-figure compensated for rejection by the mother. I had special privileges at Rodez. I was rich, and bought Ferdière's time. I should have been in a private sanatorium, but it was the war years, and I knew of Ferdière's high ratings as a new, experimental psychiatrist. He debated about whether or not to use electroshock treatments on me. Many of the psychotic patients at Rodez, including Artaud, had benefited from this innovative form of therapy. Ferdière claimed that in time Artaud might be restored to a functional, undeluded person, but whether that would affect his poetic gifts for the better or worse, he wouldn't say. Artaud was a danger to others. Ferdière told me that in an unguarded moment.

Ferdière was sufficiently pleased with my progress to consider the idea of electroshock gratuitous. He was of course insistent that I should be in therapy for a long time. I would have to resume with him on a private level, after such time as I was released from Rodez. He prolonged my stay. He said there was nowhere to go, as the war was still being fought. I was safe in the asylum. It was unlikely to be attacked should German troops mobilize an offensive on a surrendered country. He kept telling me it wouldn't be long before we all had our liberty restored. And of course, up to a point, I could play my games with him. I could sit on his lap in a tight skirt and pretend that he was Father. If I shifted position he responded involuntarily. If it hadn't been for his professional etiquette I could have reduced this man to my sexual slave. He would have become a para-father, a surrogate for my real one.

It took me an hour to get ready before going to his private study. I chose my make-up and clothes, as I would have done for Father. Ferdière prohibited my wearing a black boa or excessive jewellery. He wanted to teach me modification, and over a period of a year he persuaded me to sit opposite him in a chair, for part of my consultation. I felt acutely isolated and rejected speaking to him from a distance. My protest was to clam up. I refused to participate in our dialogue. I sat in silence for twenty, thirty, forty minutes, before he gestured that I could sit on his lap. Once there, I grew loquacious. I wanted to divulge the repertory of my sexual fantasies. I used my body as a seductive pivot, it conducted the rhythm of my speech. I took refuge in recounting the times when I had seduced my father. Or was it the other way round? Ferdière insisted on the latter; but I didn't care.

There was an acacia tree outside my bedroom window. The shadow of its feathery leaves used to sweep my pillow. The white flowers formed a pimply surf in the drive. That shadow imprinted itself on Father's back when he made love to me, or on mine when I was positioned on top of him. It came back to me as an obsessive image. Ferdière suggested we should write up out talks under the name of the acacia sessions. I believed I was in love with my psychiatrist, and at least for the space of time in which we met each week, he seemed disengaged from familial ties and exclusively my own. But try as I did, I couldn't get him to consummate our relationship. I dreamt of running away with him, of having a chauffeur-driven car take us to the south, and of our waiting for the war to end to get away. I would spend all day painting my toenails, choosing my clothes, reading erotic novels, selecting the aphrodisiacal oysters we would have in the evening, and deciding on a wine that would taste of the flintiest, most pungent of autumn vines.

I dreamt these things. In reality I was a patient who manifested symptoms of exaggerated delusion. On bad days my hallucinated past was too threateningly invasive. I was given three-monthly injections of valium. Even at Rodez I lived the life of a diva. Unable to get flowers or chocolates, I compensated with little things. I draped shawls and silk scarves over my bed. I lay on the cushions smoking, reading, dressed to go on-stage. I was a stylized anomaly amongst the mad. One of the less disturbed patients, and not kept under confinement, I formed a small circle of friends amongst the staff and patients. We all kept clear of Artaud in his moods of apocalyptic raving.

I can remember how as a girl I was terrified of an uncle who used to visit us one weekend every month. I lived for days in dread of his arrival. Like Artaud he was emaciated, his chopstick-thin arms waving in the air as he threw a red ball across the lawn for his spaniel to retrieve. It was also his way of pinning one with stalked eyes which created panic in my nerves. Artaud had a similar effect on me. He was constantly judgemental. His egomania demanded that he was the singular victim of most schemes. There was nothing fluent about his life; he was angular to every surface. It was impossible to know if it was his internal rage that generated dementia or the complex metaphysical structure he had worked out to account for his confinement. I avoided him, for the counterpart to irrational hatred is pity. I didn't want to find myself pitying this badly damaged man in the rag suits he affected with such dignity. There were too many emotions about which I was unsure. Artaud evoked unresolved areas in my psyche, and I'm sure the actor in him used these to calculated effect. He could throw me into a state of frenzied panic. If I opened the door on the inside to him, he would never go away. He would count me amongst his daughters of the heart, his potential lovers in a world about to be transformed.

Pity for me brought back the image from childhood of my being unable to prevent pets from dying, of seeing the big fear lit in the brown centre of a dog's eyes, and being powerless to reverse the gradual closing down of the body. I didn't want to open up that role to Artaud. He would have shattered me, for there was a manipulative twist to his illness, and he used it to advantage with the staff. Artaud menaced people. He claimed to possess occult powers, the nature of which frightened others into submission. He intimidated them by the source he claimed was responsible for his mental disturbance. And he must have known

137

that I realized this. His sensitivity was too magnified not to read emotions put up as defence against his implacable arrogance. We spend our lives configuring, prefiguring ways in and out of someone's head. With Artaud I had to establish a wall. Try as he did to deface it with graffiti, he couldn't get through. I too had my metaphors with which to confront him, my hypersensitively balanced emotions. My way was to avoid him. I'd turn round mid-corridor and retreat if I saw him walking my way. But he'd still try to get my attention. He'd sometimes place books outside my door intended for my reading, but I'd leave them there as disowned property for the orderlies to retrieve.

I discussed my feelings about Artaud with Ferdière. He was much in sympathy with his patient's visionary declarations, but he wanted to step up the number of shock treatments Artaud was to receive. There was a rebel in Ferdière, a doctor intent on subverting current practices of psychiatry. He was in a position of unhappy compromise. He had deserted poetry for medicine, and the configurator in him doubted the truth of both callings. I had the feeling that he was unhappy, and that if one scratched the surface an underground spring of repressed grievances would issue from his lips. I like to tell myself that he must have entertained the idea of running away with me. Travelling in an open car to the coast, releasing balloons into the slipstream and watching them waver into flight. But there was never time enough for me to extend our relationship into a deeper one. We were cramped by having to adopt the respective roles of patient and doctor. I kept thinking, just a little further and we'll arrive, a few more sympathetic tangents and we'll meet at the apex of the magic mountain, the gold tent on which mystics perched in the timelessness of vision. But I wanted his hands and his tongue, his heart and his genitals.

I was back to Father and the need to re-create him. At one time, before I became ill, I had spent weeks walking the streets looking for a man who might fit his description. I used to eye them in close-up, assimilate their characteristics like a procuress angling for flesh. I found no one worth adopting as a substitute father. They were all misshapen, flawed, holed by life. Even the most impeccable suit looked wrongly worn. An iris had too many red flecks in it; a hand lacked my father's elegant fingers. When the rare person really demanded my attention, he was always gay. I took to going to gay bars, believing incongruously that Father would suddenly materialize out of the blue smoke, a drag queen on his arm, a pink carnation tucked behind his ear. I sat on high stools, sipping cocktails that looked like expressionist paintings poured into a glass. And in my mind I was always about to go on-stage. I was dressed for the part, and I wanted it. I met men who could have adopted Father's role, if their sexual orientation hadn't been otherwise. And then I started wondering if Father wasn't partly homosexual. Was this the cause of his rift with Mother, and was this the reason for my being attracted to him?

I talked to Ferdière about my suspicions. What was the motivation that had me find refuge amongst gay men? I wasn't consciously out to convert or to find reassurance in the knowledge that I would doubtless sleep alone that night. It was something more than that. An instinctive empathy that, had I been a man, I would have been like that. Or was I looking for another angle on Father? Had I come in search of his shadow life, the one he kept underground and removed from his social identity? I fantasized about the lovers he may have taken. Perhaps they included the man talking to me across the bar about the latest Chanel fashions, or the pianist who drank blue ladies to match the sapphire he wore on his left hand.

Ferdière was abstract in his reflections on my dilemma. He quoted Freud: 'All human beings are capable of making a homosexual object choice.' He was reluctant to cast me in the role of the phallic woman, the one who fantasizes about having sex with feminine men as a substitute for unsublimated lesbianism. Nor did I entertain the wish to cross-dress. I was happy with my overpronounced femininity. I wanted to be the compulsive centre of attention. I contested repartee with drag queens I

139

admired, and was complimented in return. I chose my colours aptly, giving particular emphasis to accessories. The glass buttons I had sewn on to a black jacket rained with blue and green rhinestones attracted every eye in the bar. My silk handkerchiefs in cerise or violet colours, my feathers, face-nets, the tilt of a beret or rakish brim all contributed to my acceptance in the gay milieu. And how could I explain to my adopted ethos that I was looking for my father? That even though he was dead he might be in the back room, or expected later, a talcumed ghost pretending to be there in a black wool suit and gingham shirt, here to pick up his daughter and not a man for the night?

Little by little my inner narrative became Ferdière's property. I opened up the secret rooms in my psyche and left him to sort through the contents. His manner was implacably cool. His composure never suffered, no matter how shocking the revelations. And the more I fed him, the more there was to give. Even if I'd crossed the Sahara on foot with him, I wouldn't have had time to tell him my story. And isn't this the essential tragedy of life? None of us is ever truly heard. We hold on to things hoping they'll die with us. It's still another form of investment account, the repression of a biography in the belief that the facts will in time become disinformation. I discussed this with Ferdière. How much should we tell, and how much conceal? Is a life an open or a closed event? And what are the merits of concealment or confession? Truth and lies. But there wasn't time to deconstruct the universal system. Ferdière taught me to focus on areas of subjective anxiety, specifically and concentratedly, and to let the rest go.

It was a combination of Artaud's persecution of me, and the infatuation I had developed for Ferdière, that had me leave Rodez for a private clinic. I could feel my nerves stretched too tight. A breakdown inside might have led to a long period of clinical tedium. I couldn't risk having Artaud around me in the event of collapse. I debated the issue over a period of months, fearing each day to part with the attentions of my psychiatrist.

I knew that I would be leaving the only man who could serve as a substitute for my father. I would miss the colour of his socks, the timbre of his voice, the sensitivity that filtered through his inveterate fatigue. I had given him the story of my life. Would he place it in a box, take it to the south, and bury the container beneath sand? Would the shapely girl spread her towel over my heart and lie there bronzing all through the lazy blue afternoon? The myth would go on in my mind – July afternoons, the acacia shadows whipping my body, a tongue in my mouth tasting of champagne, the arched rhythm of my body reaching elastic configurations as I strained towards orgasm. It was like being possessed by a leopard without claws, the ejaculation firing gold stars into my body, seeds igniting galaxies in my interior. I was so elated after Father's love-making that I couldn't sleep. I would lie awake all night unwashed, as I didn't wish to lose his scent, wild to re-experience my tumultuous crisis. I would fit his body to mine in the imagination. A glove resting against another glove: a pair. Even if he was out all night, I held him in my arms. His contours moulded themselves to my girl's body.

I would have offered the same to Ferdière. His professional status kept him cold. If I had placed love-letters in his shoes, he would have extracted them as irritants. But there was a lateral shift in him towards arousal when I sat on his lap. I could feel his emotional reserve break up. His mind broke free of professional jargon, the analytical terminology he employed as part of the act of distancing. It was then I reached the responsive man in him, the one who admired the pink roses in the grounds and who sat up at night writing erotic poems charged with surreal imagery. And if I could have sat with him under the stars, listening to an owl drop, and the incisive scratch of his pen travelling across paper, I would have been happy. I would have sat and watched the nerves ignite in his face as inspiration arrived. And later I would have walked across the room in a transparent négligé and sat on his lap. The completion of the poem would mark the beginning of love. Our bodies would interlink

141

in a sinuous geometry. The night would close over us as water does over a diver.

It was predominantly Artaud's letters that precipitated my leaving. I would receive them for five consecutive days, paper burnt at the edges, the astrological and esoteric diagrams gouged into a threateningly predictive text. I trod on one and then threw away my shoes. I began to see his eyes staring at me in the dark, his face walking out of the mirror. I couldn't stand any more. His insane presence stood in every corridor. I was terrified he would surprise me in my room.

Ferdière discounted my fears. He assured me that Artaud had no record of striking fellow-patients, and that his mania was confined to scatological vitriol. But the onslaught had drained me. My aesthetic sensibility longed for suitable comforts. I refused to see Ferdière for two weeks, complaining of headaches and dispiritment.

When I finally confronted him, I told him the truth. I had to leave. I HAD to leave. I watched the colour drain from his eyes. He was shocked out of his formal manner. He looked at me from blank spaces, and then from nowhere at all. And as soon he reintegrated. He was once again my psychiatrist, solicitous that I should feel comfortable in my environment. There was a war going on, but he would see what he could do. He was naturally anxious that I should continue treatment with another doctor. I agreed to this. I was in a state in which I would have acquiesced to anything.

And the day before I left, I sat up all night making myself glamorous in preparation for my departure. I wanted them to remember me. I took out my red sequinned skirt and a matching red hat, together with a black coat. I pronounced my make-up, stepping my cheek-bones higher towards my pencilled eyebrows.

It was raining outside. The car came early. Ferdière had insisted a nurse accompany me on the journey to the sanatorium. It was his last act of protocol. He was there at the window as I went out to the car. His white shirt stood out distinctly. I wondered if his wife was watching over his shoulder. I took off a black glove and raised my hand towards him. What else could I do? There was no response, but at that moment a ray of light came through from the early sun and lit the window in the form of a star. It was gone again as I looked round frantically from the car accelerating away from the grounds and another day at Rodez.

Chapter 7

Women fall in love with me. It's part of being a psychiatrist. I remember and forget my patients, their illnesses, their obsessions, the desperation that has them exalt me to the elevated status of a healer, a mentor. But I'm none of these things. Whatever is transferred to me I disown. The freeing of psychic phenomena in the patient's mind is utilized by me for diagnostic categories. As a poet, I try to encourage creativity in my patient. I would rather the psychic extract was directed into art than killed dead by the clinical analyses of psychopathology. The urge towards individuation and the transcendant function of consciousness is one I have spent a lot of time debating. So too the relationship between madness and creativity. Is the creative drive a product of illness or a therapeutic function aimed at modifying disturbance? Or is there no causal relationship between the two?

There was a woman here, Denise X, for the sake of keeping her case history anonymous, who felt terrorized by Artaud's presence. An attractive woman in her mid-thirties, given to dressing in the manner of Greta Garbo and Marlene Dietrich, her disturbances were psychosexual. In order to compensate for a failed career on the stage she had constructed elaborate sexual fantasies which came in time to dominate and obstruct her progress. I became a part of her fictions.

And Artaud? I believed neither of them. Both suffered from hysterical delusions, and Denise adopted the obsessive belief that Artaud was persecuting her. There were other patients to whom Artaud sent spells, and I or my colleagues were quick to assure them that the content meant nothing. To most of them it was indecipherable anyhow. The coloured crayons used, and the diagrammatic nature of the text had it look like a discarded attempt at art therapy to the uninitiated. But for some reason, Denise paid close attention to the initial letters that Artaud sent. She consulted me over the meaning of symbols from the I Ching, and the prophetic quotations which Artaud had employed.

I was anxious to understate the importance of these writings. Artaud was rapacious to transpose universal symbols into terms of a private mythology. His readings of the Zohar and other related cabbalistic writings had introduced him to the origin of evil and the notion that man elected his own fall from angelic grace. The hermetica encouraged his masochistic adherence to asexuality. Fear of the physical body and the erroneous misconception that sex was a betrayal of the light and a descent into dark were characteristics of his mental state. It was impossible to shift him from these convictions. And I had no wish that Denise should become a part of Artaud's metaphysical system. His manner was to win converts by reason of the mystic powers to which he laid claim. The susceptible soon became hooked.

I wasn't won over, for all my intellectual discussion with Artaud. I found his esoteric doctrines extraneous to the man, they seemed like a desperate fabrication to support an extreme ideal. As a poet I was faced with a dilemma, one that centred on the issue of truth. Do we adopt beliefs knowing that they're untenable,

145

simply to give a structure to our lives? Do we know that there's really nothing, even in the truths we expatiate, and quite by accident choose entomology, medicine, bricklaying or even poetry as a defensive function against the fundamental mystery of being? There aren't any answers to these things. And so I doubted Artaud's self-vindicatory system. It was like a ladder which had grown from his head, and which supported nothing but his own vision of the universe. Every poet imagines he has found the secret of life, whereas in principle he has discovered his own sense of difference. What I wanted was not for Artaud to lose his vision, but for him to feel less contentiously isolated. He was unable to produce sustained work because his energies were eroded by continual conflict with every aspect of life. At Rodez, he at least had a secure place in which to live, for he was incapable of earning. His antagonism to life made him unemployable. He fell out with friends, and preferred to live with the idea of their forming a perfect circle of protection. His life was a retreat into solitude. He was too fascinated by his hallucinations to modify these for relationships. Artaud's past was one in which interested women were rejected for their physical designs on his body. We never discussed the problems of impotence, but I suspect they were an issue. The amount of drugs he had taken would have killed off anyone's libido. He had come to equate the sexual impulse with Satanism.

Denise X represented the scarlet woman in his terminology. He saw her as a temptress, a reminder of his dealings with the Paris theatre and women he had unsuccessfully pursued. He was offended by her disregard for his presence as a writer and person. He expected to be recognized on the strength of unpublished work, and believed that hundreds of thousands of copies of his few small books had been sold in Paris. Initially Denise had played games with him. She was fascinated and repelled by his person, and every bit as demanding of attention as Artaud. She expected to be revered for her artistic aspirations and received contempt from Artaud who was diligent in his concern for truth. Neither had the reputation to which they laid claim

146

subjectively, and both fantasized about fame. Artaud would have liked the inordinate power of a decadent Roman emperor, his fictional re-creation of Heliogabalus's life being a work of considerable empathy, and Denise wanted to play Olympia and offer her elbow-length red gloves to the audience. They developed a mutual hostility based on feelings of disrespect; only Artaud with his obsessive behavioural patterns went further. He decided to victimize this woman as someone in part responsible for his illness and internment. He claimed that prior to Denise's arrival at Rodez he was free of hallucinations. He was here by way of a bureaucratic error. And that after she took up residence at Rodez, he was once again subject to head pains and confused by demonic intervention. He wanted at the time to run for president or be elected as the supreme European leader. He told me that he had received instructions from the police and the army to take up his position. Denise was to design him a gold suit; he would be revealed in his true identity.

Although my duties were demanding, and I treated all patients with equal care, I found myself devoting more time to Artaud as a person than any other inmate or private patient. It wasn't just the connection with Robert Desnos who had been instrumental to his coming here, it was more the compelling nature of Artaud's extremism that had me spend long hours in his company. Artaud had constructed a monocentric universe, but one sufficiently flawed to allow evil to penetrate. To account for the latter he continued to invent the elaborate myth which comprised his madness. But I wasn't prepared just to listen, I treated him not unsuccessfully with medicine. He had been catatonic before coming to me, and I was instrumental in re-energizing his creative faculties.

Artaud also had the notion of inventing a new body, one which would function by electric impulses alone and be independent of physical organs. He was impatient to experience this in his lifetime, he wanted to be free of ingestion, assimilation, metabolization, excretion. He wanted to live with nothing but a network of nerves which communicated with the stars. In retro-

147

spect one can see that he was anticipating the work done by Brion Gysin and William Burroughs towards establishing dream machines and a metamorphic autonomy for a mind conditioned to experimental drugs. Artaud believed in the indestructibility of consciousness, but at the same time this increased his morbid awareness of the body's dissolution. It was an area of study that interested me. Drugs had been used in every society which placed an emphasis on collective vision. The prophetic, the shamanistic, the oneiric were all directly linked to the taking of drugs. Baudelaire, Poe, Nerval and Rimbaud had turned instinctively to hallucinogens to stimulate a vital imagination. Artaud rightly blamed the capitalist system for attempting to repress vision. The predominant concerns of the nineteenth and twentieth century have been the acquisition of corporate and individual wealth at the expense of all inner concerns. Poets have particularly suffered at the hands of a material society, and Artaud took up the cause of vision in opposition to materialism, truth in contention with fraud. The poet in me responded to this singular quest. It is invariably left to the committed individual to point a road to the future, even if flames rip up its surface.

We had all lost touch with the war. I suspect Artaud attached no importance to it as an event; he was preoccupied solely with the inner, and the evolution of consciousness. If I had told my patients that France was occupied it wouldn't have registered as significant. Denise was sufficiently concerned with external events to know of the possible national danger involved, but I kept the political situation away from my patients. There was too much to be done on an inner level, and electroshock treatment was proving beneficial to the clinically depressed. It was an important time for psychiatry. I was convinced that the truths inherent in madness could be attuned to coherent communication, and I was determined to bring Artaud to that level. Blake had managed to prevent his vision becoming pathological, and I hoped Artaud would find a similarly constructive manner of focusing his energies. He professed gratitude for the interest that I and my colleagues showed in his health, but his moods still tended

148

to oscillate between taking excrement into the chapel and piously asking to attend confession.

Denise kept to her room, or was allowed into my private library where she read or listened to music. I had to keep this distance between us. I would find her arranged in a chair, revealing too much leg and touching up her eyes or lips in a compact mirror. She left the air scented with her walk. She was the archetypal feminine, but dissolute, shot through with perverse sexual fantasies. I had accompanied her on a deep enough journey to the interior to be sure that her stories of voluntary incest were true. The erotic confessions of this sophisticated young woman were told unflinchingly. To heighten her life and demand the excessive attention denied her she had experimented with all forms of sex. Her appetite at times approached nymphomania. She encouraged taxi-drivers to have her on the back seat, she had made love in reference libraries; she had allowed men to pick her up in the street and take her to cheap hotels, or lift her expensive skirt at the dead end of an alley. She had experienced little pleasure from these casual encounters. What she demanded was the individual attention they never gave her: she wanted to be seen to be special. We were careful to ensure that no sexual liaison between her and the inmates occurred at Rodez. She seemed happy to treat me as a surrogate father, but one who conformed to the familial taboo surrounding incest.

But her stories, I repeat, were extraordinary. She told me of a librarian who used to visit her in the evenings, and how she would place him in leather handcuffs and allow him to advance up her thighs only at the progress of one inch an hour. He would have to start just above her knees, and she would lift her skirt to correspond to his progress. She had long legs, and it would take him eight or nine hours to reach her crotch, but such was his desperation to make love to her that he would undergo the ordeal. By the time he arrived at his destination, he was desperate. He would fall on her and take her ferociously. And in the course of this prolonged game she would read him a book of his choice.

149

Her stories, whether they were authentic or fantastic, were always original. I gave them the credibility of truth. There were no traces of psychosis or pathological mendacity in this woman. She was someone who, unsuited to the life with which she identified, had created an alternative reality. She continually offered her beauty to men who were insensitive to that faculty. Denise was in search of someone who would recognize her, know her for the frustrated singer who lived in her psyche. She told me of how she had waited outside stage doors expecting to be noticed, she had auditioned for parts and been rejected. She had walked through the nights in sequins or velvet, a nocturnal myth to the few on the streets.

I listened over the months and over the course of a year to her fragmented narrative. The romantic in her thankfully would never be silenced. There was also something extraordinary about the attention she gave her appearance. She had stocked up on make-up so excessively that the war scarcities didn't affect her. I never saw her without false eyelashes, gloss lipstick, foundation, painted fingernails. She was neurotically fastidious and treated her face like a painter, brushes in hand pigmenting the tone of her facial planes, darkening or lightening her lips, lifting her cheek-bones by the application of highlights.

Denise was individual to the point of having created herself. She would have stood out anywhere. I had to bring her back to a tangent which intersected with reality. I feared that without clinical attention she would end up abused or murdered. Her promiscuity gravitated towards a pronounced death-wish. Her exhibitionism was sacrificially masochistic. She would have had sex on the scaffolding boards above a busy high street if she thought it would attract sufficient attention. And, what's more, she would have had sex with me anywhere at any time. Do I keep my own secrets? Perhaps the essence of a life is better kept ambiguous. What happened between us in those hours of consultation and leisure is already an event of the past.

Denise liked her body. Her legs were one continuous curve from the hips to the ankles. I tried to rationalize the situation

150

over Artaud, but she was unrelenting. I couldn't shift her fixated belief that he was persecuting her through his mental and written communications. Her way of drawing up a screen was to take her lipstick out of her handbag and concentrate on linear embellishments, thickening the width of the lower lip, so as to create a bow with the upper. And of course it worked. The inevitable pout would follow, before she directed the conversation to a disjunctive field. I realized anyhow that I had gone beyond etiquette in extending personal friendships to both Denise and Artaud, but it was my method of approach. I couldn't clinically objectify the individual lives of two people whom I valued as friends, although I continued to treat them as patients. I wanted Rodez to be a place where staff and inmates formed an interdependency rather than a militated separation of powers. It wasn't easy. The myth that the insane are frustrated geniuses often rendered incoherent by social opposition is true of the few, but not of the many. Random groups of vowels and consonants, such as Artaud formulated by way of a new language, are not an easy method of communication. Inarticulacy was common among our patients, there's always the theory advanced that language fails to accommodate experience, and that its limitations are etymological rather than experiential, and Artaud's particular chemical imbalance resulted in a chaotic system of signs. He started writing poems in this invented language, but I stopped him. He had taken on enough of the world without falling out of an inherited language. Artaud's problem was that he expected immediate comprehension of his methods from the reader, and felt rejected when his work failed to be granted the privileges accorded the conventional. He wanted to be new and yet judged by the standards of the old.

I was worried too about the incipient hysteria Denise showed whenever I mentioned Artaud's name. Her retreat was into a world of protective fantasy. Father would reappear, and so too would the idea of her red stilettos on the boards. I would lose her to the dual world from which I had been attempting to extract her, and I couldn't risk a serious relapse on her part. I decided, much against my wishes, that she should be transferred to a private clinic. We would correspond, and there were plans for future meetings. I prepared her for the change over a number of weeks, and predictably Artaud's attentions to her lessened. He must have sensed that he had her in a position of retreat.

Denise and I met for a last time in my study prior to the day of her departure. As always, she was overdressed. She wore a red hat with a spotted black face-net. Her false fingernails had a scarlet finish. She was theatrically sad. She sat with her left profile tilted towards me, her legs visible beneath a skirt split to the thigh. Above her head were my copies of books by Proust, Breton, Éluard, Aragon, Tzara, and their mentors Lautréamont, Rimbaud and Sade. I had a statuette of a hermaphrodite Apollo placed on the table that divided us. I was reflective, my mind was on poetry and chance – the random sign that points one way instead of another and briefly determines the future. How many loves could each of us have? Are there alternative wives to the one wife, and is it habit that prevents us from changing? I threw these questions like a juggler's balls into the air, knowing I had no answers. And was death also a game of chance?

Denise was excluded from my inner preoccupations until I got back to the immediate. And I saw truly for the first time how beautiful she was as a woman, and how the light stayed in the upper planes of her face, while her eyes were in shadow. She crossed her legs with consummate poise. There was so much unspoken, despite the closeness of our doctor/patient relationship. In a way there was no point in beginning to cross those great deserts of reserve that comprise the individual psyche. I wanted her to leave easily, optimistically, positive about the inner knowledge she had gained from her stay here. I was already seeing her as another patient who had come and gone. Some keep in touch and write from time to time, others disappear into the crowd. The territory was fragile. Denise was looking for comfort I didn't dare offer. It was the first time she hadn't come to sit on my lap, and I had the feeling that she was asking me to look at what I was losing, evaluate the consequences of rejecting a relationship.

As I sat confronting her, an image from my childhood returned. I was going away to boarding-school for the first time, and the black cat which was my pet watched me get into my father's car with visible disquiet. Its eyes were banged out like yellow moons. Whatever psi energy connected us was being transmitted as panic. As my father pulled away from the house, the cat darted behind us for the length of the road. I looked back once and saw its impossibly desperate eyes and then we were gone. But the image stayed with me. It punched a hole into my brain that would never heal.

I could feel the silence stretch wings against the walls. The situation was loaded, and I couldn't risk a patient throwing an emotive scene. Who was this woman who felt so deeply that she had accepted solitude and institutionalization for lack of the right person to replace her father? In my mind I saw her walk through all the cities of the world in search of this dead man, refusing in the process what was offered her to begin again. She would carry a rose in one hand, an urn full of ashes in the other. She would stay in the best hotels, always alone, the bed heaped with her costumes. Her story would be told by countless porters, desk-clerks, taxi-drivers. She would be the woman they never knew, the one always in transit between appointments. Wouldn't they see her giving away money in the street to children, scrutinizing men but never seeking their company, and capriciously deciding in the middle of the night to have a car take her to the airport for a dawn flight? Bills would be settled while the hotel slept, and no matter the hour her make-up would always be perfect, her clothes pressed as though they had never been worn. I could invent a future for this enigmatic woman and feel assured that it would be fulfilled. But before these things could be realized it was necessary that she undergo treatment.

Denise kept her face in profile. She was acting out the degree of her hurt. She was visibly mourning her departure. I tried to switch her round to the idea of a future in which the pathologized

153

image of her dead father would be better assimilated with her life. I spoke of the need to reduce the pharmaceuticals she was taking, and of how she would benefit by coming off barbiturates. I got on to the subject of novels, poetry, the extraordinary mauve and pink petunias which were proliferating in the window-boxes, the hopes we all entertained of the war coming to an end. Denise delayed, then turned to face me slowly, inching the right side of her face into view, and as she completed the action I saw she had made her face up to resemble two different people. Her right eyebrow was pencilled thickly, the left was raised and imperceptibly thin, the right eye was a black almond of eye-liner and mascara, the left was dusted bronze; there was blusher on the right cheek and not on the left, scarlet lipstick on the upper and lower right side of the lips, and bright pink on their counterparts. I was thrown by the visual effects. Used theatrically, Denise's innate exhibitionism employed a vocabulary which questioned the whole issue of sexuality.

She looked clearly and deliberately into my eyes, searching to note the shift in my perception, presenting me with her cosmetic duality, and at the same time arching a leg so that the sole of her right foot rested on the left knee, her sheer stocking breathing in the give at the knee, a mauve shoe dangling from her foot. The pulse in me jumped at the sight of her displayed legs, but inwardly I was following the distraction of watching camels head off at dawn from an oasis, the sun-blackened Arthur Rimbaud somewhere amongst that team, shivering with fever, cursing the fate that brought him there to be ruined, the gesture of his fist raised to the sky impressing on him how diminutive is the human stature against its vastness.

I kept with that train of thought while Denise settled to a less provocative position. Her thoughts were coming from a long way away. She was looking at them like someone watching a film. I was waiting for her to share some of the more persistent images. She was sunk deep into herself. 'I'm thinking of a time in my life when I waited each day for something to happen,' she said. 'I mean, I really expected whatever it was to arrive. A

154

person, a thing, a detail small but complete as a moth, or more representationally a box wrapped in blue paper which I expected to find outside the front door, waiting for me. I would go and check that site twenty or thirty times a day, and sometimes in the night as well. I got to a point whereby I wouldn't have known the difference between imagining it and claiming it as a reality. I was confused. One night I believed I had the blue box in my arms. I carried it upstairs, not even conscious of its weight, just wild to have the thing in my possession. I placed the box on the bed and stood there looking at it for a long time. It didn't move, but it seemed to transmit light like the rays of a star. I knew then that I couldn't open it. I had to imagine what was inside. And a whole string of possibilities invaded my mind. I told myself that it might contain the shape of the future in the form of an envelope containing the wind's tail. Or it might hold a ring that Father had chosen for me in death, or a scarab lifted from a pyramidal burial chamber. I asked myself what it was I needed so badly to complete my life. There was some component of unity that I lacked. I was a two-sided triangle. I kept my distance from the blue box. I knew if I touched it, it would disappear. It was like chancing my future to violate the thing's perfection.

'I lit a cigarette to convince myself I wasn't dreaming, and felt the pungent smoke curl into the roof of my mouth. I bit the tobacco and tasted its sharp tang. I wasn't sleeping. I stood in front of the mirror and noted my reflection. I was wearing the black silk négligé I had so often worn for my father. It was slashed open to the hips, he had bitten through the spaghetti straps so the upper part hardly concealed my breasts. It was me, Denise. I was sure of that and nothing else.

'There was a wind outside in the tall poplars, I could see them all point one way in a sustained flurry. Sound isn't a part of my dreams. Once I had found myself being pursued on horseback to the lip of a thundering waterfall which smoked at the bottom of the abyss, but I had heard nothing. I heard the poplars. It was like the roar of surf in the night sky. And then I went on

155

looking. The box was bluer. It was like a cube cut out of the sky and deposited on my bed. To touch it would have been to vandalize the contents. I conceived of a pure image being inside, bright like the jeweller's concept before he commits the stone to his craft. It could have represented the mystery of life, the pristine atom of creation.

'I was excited and terrified. I found myself pursuing my usual idiosyncrasy of putting on lipstick before making a decision. I made myself up and returned to guessing. I had the notion that if I selected the right image, the sequence would click and the box would open itself. I would be freed of that responsibility. I thought of a sea-horse, a gold apple, a diminutive father inside a mauve egg, a ring that spoke, an angel's wing. My mind crystallized possible inclusions. But nothing worked. I felt the same sort of gap between me and it as I do when thinking about my own death.

'I decided to leave the room and pour myself a drink. I walked through corridors, the house lit up like a ship on night waters. I drank a brandy and tried to come to a decision. My mind hummed with big thoughts which wouldn't settle. They were like bees bugging a peach. I had to get it right, and I couldn't. Images proliferated. Had someone sent me Father's head? The box wasn't heavy enough. A hand, a foot? The box was too light. It had to be something else. I was distracted. Was this really me, strung out in the early hours of the morning, my lips stung by brandy, vacillating over a quandary which could decide my future?

'I went back upstairs, completing a mental journey which seemed to occupy centuries. I hesitated outside my bedroom door, as a gambler would in displaying his last card. The sky dropped down to sit on my shoulders. I went back into the room with my mind disconcertingly blank, and the box had disappeared. I looked at the space it had occupied expecting the thing to rematerialize. Nothing. There was a warmth imparted to the counterpane where the box had rested. I kept running my hands over that site. I went over to the window and looked outside. I was half expecting to see it lying on the lawn or lodged in the trees. But there was only the blank cobalt of the night. Not a sound, the wind had died out. The neighbouring houses had their lights extinguished. There was nothing to qualify my belief that the box had existed. I was desperate that I may have imagined the whole thing. I kept closing my eyes, believing that when I opened them again the object would be there. I lay there sleepless and profoundly disillusioned. I felt that I had lost the opportunity to resolve the fundamental enigma at the centre of my being. What you call psyche.

'I spent the post-dawn hours sitting up staring at a spot I couldn't reimagine as a box. I couldn't even visualize my loss as an image. I was desperate. I felt I had missed the purpose of my life, and that even in death I would go on searching for that lost object. I continued to sit on the bed all day, in a state of mourning. I felt I had refused my father's gift. He had sent it by way of a messenger from death. Why else would it suddenly be placed outside the front door in the middle of the night? Meteors drop out of the sky. So do special gifts. And, if you like, that was the beginnings of my breakdown. If I told this to anyone else they would assume I was mad. But you as a poet know these things happen. Isn't inspiration the gift for which there's no accounting? The faculty that jumps into the head without the intervention of the hands? If anything brought me to seek help it was this occurrence. There aren't explanations. You, Dr Ferdière, can either tell me that the experience was imagined or real. Neither will assure me.'

I let Denise follow her drift. She looked away from me, and took off one glove, and then another.

'The problems with all analysis are that subject and therapist are inalienably separated by the formal structure of consultation. I can tell you this. There's never a chance of the two coming together sufficiently to allow for accidental confession. I mean the imparting of secrets in the way of lovers, where whole areas of life may be reclaimed by a chance association. You and I have never achieved this. I suspect you've never got that far with any of your patients. It's not a criticism. It's a truth. Who can we expect this from? Who will jolt the deepest secrets from their unconscious strata? We are lucky if we ever find love – beyond that there's no knowing. It saddens me that we will never realize this in each other. There's something twisted about imparting secrets intended for a lover to a dispassionate observer. But I've done it voluntarily.'

I didn't interrupt Denise. She was placing me on the same edge as other female clients had attempted to establish. I was expected to offer love in return for psychic transference. Some analysts fulfil that role. I let Denise continue her story.

'When I'm free of clinical help, what will become of me then? My needs won't have diminished, and there'll be no one there to listen. Only the gay men I take back from bars, to watch them dress up in my clothes, express themselves through my eye-shadows, mascara and lipstick. I'll be too lonely. I'll continue my search in foreign cities for my dead father. I'll expect to find him sitting on a hotel terrace, or browsing in a bookshop for novels to appease his insatiable sexual curiosity. I'll buy him a new shirt, a wine from the year that he favours. We'll be booked in a hotel suite for a week. And if I don't find him, I'll have lost you too. It's not clinics I need, it's attention, love.'

'We can write to each other, so that I have news of your progress,' I volunteered, aware of the objective note I assumed when talking to a patient. But my feelings for Denise were ambivalent. Part of me dreaded her departure, and yet the clinical side of me felt relieved to be dispatching a patient who I felt had made sufficient progress to move on. I wanted to avoid the subject of Artaud, but Denise seemed intent on reinforcing the victimization she had suffered at his hands.

'Why do you give Artaud such privileges? Everyone knows he should be in a strait-jacket. You allow him to menace people like myself, and then you condone his violence on the grounds that he's a poet. I have never in my life encountered someone so obscenely threatening. Did you know that he smeared his

158

excrement on my door, and that he warned me he would deposit it under my pillow? Sometimes I couldn't enter my room for fear he had executed his threat. And you allow this to go on. None of the other disturbed patients ever treated me with this sort of contempt. He hates women. His misogyny is unrelenting. I could have been one of his spiritual daughters, he had the audacity to tell me. It's to exorcize him from my life that I'll be glad to be gone. I would like to have rehabilitated here, but that madman runs between my feet like a rat. He's an obstruction to recovery. He thinks he is god, and that he's in combat with demonic forces who intend to subvert his creation. You may explain it like that, but you're removed from his ravings. He ties himself up in cord and shrieks like a bird in the corridor. He may be acting out his madness, but what of the others?'

I avoided rising to Artaud's defence. I didn't want to make him into a subject of contention now that Denise was departing. Nor do I have to justify my treatment of individuals. I let it go, and she continued, though as a sign of her displeasure she returned to presenting a profile.

'You'll never believe the effect that his spells had on me. These burnt texts with their symbolic drawings and portentous scrawl. That sort of thing seeps into the recipient, just as it's intended to do. It was like having a black widow planted on my bed. Never in my life will I forget these incidents, and yet you're quite prepared to allow them to continue. When I'm gone, it will be someone else he persecutes. Whatever his gifts may be, they don't justify his actions. I don't care whether he thinks he's Napoleon or Hitler, I won't be psychologically maltreated in this way. You're so sure that he won't offer violence to other patients, but I'm not. He could end up murdering someone on a day he's convinced that he's Heliogabalus making a triumphant entry into Rome. He's twisted, perverted and malicious. But he's your star patient.'

Denise swung back to full facial. My eyes ran up her skirt as she adjusted her sitting position. She was suddenly a little girl again, pouting, the woman in her coming through in the pro-

159

vocativeness of the gesture. She wanted my attention, she needed me once again to be her father. And once again I presented a blank.

'This may be the last time we'll speak,' she continued. 'I don't belong here. I want to go early tomorrow, without attracting the notice of the other patients. I shouldn't have been here this long, anyway. I chose to stay on because I considered you were the person best qualified to help me. But you feel more comfortable with Artaud's dementia. It's probably more of a challenge to you than my singular obsession. Perhaps you think there's a way out of his problem, but not so for mine. I shall wear black tomorrow. My eyes will be black, and my face veiled. Someone looking out of a window will see me. They will call me the black bride, the woman who is married to death. You can understand this. My relations are with the dead. And every man I take back with me is in the hope that beneath his makeup I will find my father's face. His features will come clear of the mask. I sometimes have the idea that he's in hiding from me, and that another man is concealing his eyes, his nose, his lips. But no sooner have I touched their faces, stared deeply into their eyes, traced a cold finger over their lips, than I abruptly leave. Once I am certain they are not hiding Father's face, I have no use for them. They return to being undistinguished strangers in the crowd. They who have anticipated love, receive immediate rejection. And it's unlikely that I'll desist from these habits. The sadism of these gestures is an uncurtailable search for truth. In a year from now, if you think of me, I'll most probably be doing this. Destroying men for pretending to be my father.'

I listened to Denise's confessions, distressed that she should obdurately resist all manner of helping herself. My sessions with her took on a negative value in the light of her intentions, although I discerned that she was perversely trying to hurt me for not taking her side against Artaud. She was deconstructing the sensitive fabric we had built during months of psychological exploration. Patients had done this to me before, devalued the psychic content of a shared journey. Again, I let it go. I was anywhere as Denise took up her theme.

'It's the irreversibility of things that poisons life. The death of one person leaves the other incomplete. The snake's head and tail never meet again. We're expected to go on living as survivors. I haven't contacted my mother once in thirty-five years. I speak to my father constantly. I could get one parent on the telephone, but I prefer my telepathic communications. Father is waiting for me. My mother is probably out buying shoes on her husband's credit. My leaving won't put an end to such thoughts. The only difference is that you won't be there to be my confidant. And will my new psychiatrist be shocked by my revelations? He'll have my case notes, but what do words mean? They're just the passive literature which attempts to clarify my emotions. Feelings aren't words. They're something else, and psychiatry attempts to substitute words for associative emotions. I'd like to reinvent myself. If I have to go on living, I'd wish to be someone less conscious of pain. And this pain be extracted from me like an irritant, a black pearl? Can I wake up as the invention of Denise? These are questions you should be putting to me. Am I not out-analysing the analyst? Are you not reliant on taking up the theme? I am always looking for answers when there are only questions. I suppose we leave death alone because there are neither questions nor answers. Only an abstract silence.'

'You are asking for unconditional freedom,' I replied. 'But none of us is ever free. Birth commits us to a chain of responsibilities, one of which is being alive, from which we never do escape. Death is not something I can confirm other than as a state of consciousness.'

I found myself taking up my characteristic exegeses, but there was something hollow about my convictions. I wanted for the first time to be free of Denise. I wanted to be alone and centred in my mind, in the way that a fish is often suspended central to a rock-pool. Denise kept repositioning herself as though her body were the various parts of a theatre. She arched her torso so that her breasts strained against the yoke of her silk blouse. She placed

161

her hands behind the back of her head, she was the actress with an imaginary audience. She kicked off her shoes and wiggled her stockinged toes.

'Don't you see,' she said, 'that the dead are simply displaced. Most people give up on them, consign them to abstract regions of space, designate them as belonging elsewhere. But that's not so. In a way they've died in order to come closer. We have them in our heads, and so it's easier to talk to them, be with them, become them. I have the feeling that I'll wake up one day as my father. And then the process will be reversed, I'll occupy his head. It's not impossible. If I meditated, I could be with him all day. As it is, I dress to please him. I wear the shoes he likes, the scarlet bras he preferred on me, the make-up he liked. He is inside me and warns away potential lovers. He will hand me over only to the right person, and then there'll be three of us. I had hoped that you were that person. But I leave tomorrow jealously protected by my father.'

I was beginning to be conscious of time. My duties lay elsewhere in the coming hour. I had to let this woman go, with all her fragility, her obsessive love, her ultimate trust in reinstating her father in her life. I was losing my sense of detachment, and my compassion for her unrequited love was dangerous in the circumstances. Her perfume had become an ambient fixture in my study. It had come to catch me by surprise when I was reading or just browsing amongst my thoughts. It was the essence by which Denise would continue to live here. If I stayed on at Rodez, I knew it would continue to catch me out, – a year, two years, five from now, an associative memory would come alive on a hint of scent, and prick me into an awareness of this woman being somewhere in the world, hunting amongst strangers for her elusive father. I would miss the flamboyance of her clothes, her lyric sensitivity to the small things in life, her captivating eloquence. Very few of my patients have ever been as articulate as Denise. Most lose clarity in illness and cannot properly describe their inner fantasies. Denise and Artaud differ in that respect. Both give coherent voice to their sufferings, Denise through a method of disarming lucidity, and Artaud through the powers of somatic invective.

I got up from my chair and walked over to the window that looks on to the grounds. A few of the inmates were out walking on the lawn, a white-coated orderly in attendance. The roses were overblown. Big crimson turbans, the first raindrop would explode their overloaded corollas. Time was standing still. It was like a surrealization of the landscape into a painting to see a patient with a motor disorder knee-jerk his way across the lawn. My profession had taken me to the involuntarily bizarre. I officiated over the madness that Rimbaud, and after him Breton, had prescribed for the poet. I felt compelled to go on looking, despite the fact that I had turned my back on Denise. I was staring at aspects of my life, the film showing at that moment recapturing incidents, fragments, details compounded from my years of Rodez. It was odd, realizing that this moment would never be again and yet had to fall in the pattern of my life. There were slow clouds stacked like sculptures on the skyline. Two rooks were gutturally declaiming from a tree-top. The mad were at play on the lawn. I was a part of this, but only if I consciously integrated myself into the sequence.

When I turned round, Denise was standing up ready to go. She was in profile, head lowered, her gloved hands folded one over the other. It was like she was waiting backstage before going on, keying herself up to the adrenalin charge in the air, feeding her own part internally before committing it to performance. I walked over towards the door. Her theatricality was impeccable. She took off one satin glove and offered me her hand. I couldn't see her eyes. She was cut off in her own mood. I found myself mechanically opening the door, and then I listened to the staccato click of her heels as she crossed the passage to connect with the main building. I went back to my desk. The book I had been reading was shut. There was something trailing from the pages. I opened it and found one of Denise's silk stockings placed in there as a marker. It was still warm, the fragile cocoon scented with her familiar perfume. I bunched it into my hand and felt the black breath settle. She must have slipped off her stockings while I had been lost at the window. This was her last sensuous reminder. I brushed it against my lips and cheeks, then concealed it in my drawer. I had patients to see. Poems to write. And, somehow, a life to live.

Chapter 8

In a month I shall leave Rodez and return to life in Paris. After so long a period of confinement I shall live fast to make up for lost time. A decade has gone into my being clinically assessed, given diagnostic tags, shot down on every form of sedative. All the time I have been waiting to unleash my subversive energies on a society that values literature as a form of media by-product. It is not only my hand that I use as the instrument of my rage, it is also my diaphragm, my thorax, my glottis, the whole instrumentalization of my voice. I am my own creation. I shall confront the public with the prototype of a new species. Artaud is the beginning and the end, the definition of non-linear progeny.

I have been working furiously for months. Ferdière ascribes this to the stimulus gained from electroshock, but for me it has to do with my need to prepare the way for the future. My work will justify my position as the leader of a new race. When I wave from a closed car, all the statues in Paris will also salute. An oracular voice will come out of the river, it will wade to the shore on webbed feet and hang there in a glitter of green air. Spiders will turn themselves inside out and be transformed into rubies. A woman will walk through the streets in a wedding dress and be married to a white horse left over from Revelation. My coming will be accompanied by so many signs in the city.

And what occupies me? The suffering of two men placed outside artistic conventions: Lautréamont and Van Gogh. I have absorbed them empathetically. I have worked my way into their neurochemistries. I defend them as one who has suffered similar injustices. I turn over in my mind the possible causes of Lautréamont's death in contradistinction to what history tells us. Was he really discovered dead by a hotel manager? Why was the proprietor drawn to visit his room? If Lautréamont hadn't been seen for days, the possibilities of murder or suicide are very real. Nowhere in his surviving letters is there mention of his ill-health or the genetic inheritance of disease. What was he wearing when he was discovered dead? Did he come into this world simply to give us *Maldoror*, and that was it? Did he die of autocombustion, his blackened body burnt out at the core? I go on asking these things. While a poet is alive, he is too powerful for people to touch. They avoid him. When he is dead, society can translate him into something modified by conventions. The live wire is insulated. Academe conveniently devaluates the power of Baudelaire, Lautréamont and Rimbaud. It separates the man from the work. It asks that we excuse madness in the interests of art. It attempts to castrate imaginative power at its source. Lautréamont was an affirmation that the word vibrates with cosmic tremors. He is designated mad without any clinical evidence to justify this contention. It is rather that he represented truth. And for Van Gogh it was the same. His life and work were unacceptable to bourgeois standards.

It is my belief that psychiatry was invented by a society seeking to defend itself against the claims of visionaries whose findings disturbed it. Madness is the pejorative term that capitalism applies to vision. Van Gogh's implosive detonations resituate natural objects. He gives simple things the weird spin of neurotic ten-

166

sion. Van Gogh committed suicide because his doctor represented not genius but the wish to silence and normalize the visionary faculty. His colours vibrate with shock impulses. His landscapes are charged with the electricity of a man whose natural momentum was to overreach. And every day of his life he must have questioned, am I an artist? Wouldn't I be better suited to doing something else, a job which wouldn't involve a confrontation with society? All true creativity comes from the tension implied by this inner dilemma. It is the untalented who assume their work has a rightful place in contemporary expression. Van Gogh painted at a shift from seeing. He articulated a world that people usually know only in moments of acute crisis, when dislodgement from circadian rhythms results in hallucinated terror.

I work on these texts with a cause. Dare I repeat the conviction I maintain? 'No one has ever written or painted, sculpted, modelled, built, invented, except to get out of hell.' When madness advances across the page, even the ink takes flight. Lakes close in on themselves, houses move back, trees change from summer to autumn in the space of seconds. I have known it. I have seen the oaks at Rodez turn red for an hour in mid-June, when I have been concentrated on poetry.

The days advance, I am told there has been an auction of manuscripts and paintings in Paris, to pay a little for my future. Ferdière insists that some form of trust has been established to provide for my needs. A war has come and gone, leaving Europe ravaged. The other Europe. Not the one that lives inside me. I have protected my capital. Its corridors lead under ruins, death camps, the remains of pogroms, the annihilation of races, and communicate with a black sun in the underworld. I know if I advance through those nocturnal tunnels I shall find Baudelaire in conversation with Poe. I shall come across a white owl narrating the thousand and one orphic nights. I shall find the mirror in which I am transformed into disincarnate being. It will happen at the speed of a photographer's flash. Pain will be something I have left behind in the way a swimmer walks free of his clothes and projects a naked body into the blue sea. I am pre-

167

paring a map of my labyrinth, but first I have to fulfil my calling in Paris. The times are right, and I am awaited.

The mystique surrounding my disappearance from life, the disseminated injustices done to me in asylums, the attraction that a new generation of writers feel for my ideas, all of these things have combined to make my work possible. It is my physical health that declines. The internal haemorrhages I have suffered, the metabolic irregularities caused by periods of drug withdrawal, the bad chemicals, electroshock convulsions. I wear my damage like someone who has survived a very different war. I am dusty with ash from the abyss. How much further?

Let me revive a memory. As a child, and before I was carved by the Marseille pimp, singled out for my mission, I was taken to the countryside with my brothers. My father was away on business as usual. My mother and a friend took us by train out of the city to woodland. She had prepared a picnic. I can see it still, the red and white chequered table-cloth spread on the grass, the gold baguettes and cratered cheeses, the purple stain on the wine cork when it was drawn. There were little blue butterflies twinkling in the grass, and crisp bees crackling in the clover. I could smell summer. Scent hung in the air like a numbing intoxicant. It pushed one down into the grasses face up to stare at a cloudless blue sky. After eating, everyone lay back, abandoned to the sun. I drowsed in and out of consciousness, too restless to submit to sleep, and seeing that no one was likely to notice, I moved off quietly into the trees. My mother's friend had spoken of the existence of a quarry nearby, and of the deep, clear pool at its base. I wanted to swim and embrace that cool. And when I found it, tearing myself on brambles to reach the green lapidary oval, I was stunned into reflection. When I looked into the water I seemed to telescope into the depths of my mind and discover thoughts swarming there, rather than fish. I jabbed a finger into the water, and the cold attached itself to me like a ring. The silence was compacted to meditation point.

I was fifteen minutes away from my family, but at the same time separated from them like someone who is dying is isolated from those who gather in the room. There was no longer any connecting information. I went on staring, compelled to follow myself out of myself. The pool was narrow but deep. And as I stared, a different reflection waded across the sheen to meet me. It wasn't my own image astrally projecting, it was someone else's elongated torso and blurred head that swatted my own. I didn't dare look up. The person was wearing red, the refracted accordion of a shirt quivered in pleats on the surface, I was afraid. My legs wouldn't move, my heart beat like an athlete's even though I was standing still. I expected this reflection to swallow mine like a giant pike risen from the depths. The two images lay across each other like fishing-lines that had got tangled. Red into my white. When I dared to look up, physically lifting the weight of my eyes, he was there in a red shirt and black shorts, a young man probably in his early twenties. He threw a stone at me, one, two, three, then clattered away over the rocks, a figure so menacing that I stood there cold, paralysed by what had happened. When I alerted myself to what had really occurred, I was terrified. I ran back through the woods, my mind big with fear, and returned to the picnic circle. I had learnt the question of my vulnerability in the face of the universe. I had realized the threat implied by others.

I lay down in the warm grass, my heart still pounding, aware that this experience would never go away. It had become a part of my consciousness. It was written into me, as it is today at the moment of writing. The figure is there again, intent on harm, but running away after having delivered a gesture of attack. This act of aggression was the precursor to the violence I received in Marseille. Was it the same figure who later on stabbed me? I shall never know, but I feel it is probable. This stranger knew me. He had singled me out. When he found me again he tried to kill me. In my dark hours I think of that. I nurse my wound. It was the mark that was the beginning of my greatness and my downfall. Neither my brothers nor my mother could extricate me from the oppressive mood that accompanied me all afternoon. I was changed, and the thing couldn't be reversed. The solution had entered my veins. Never again could I be just a child.

Nothing interested me for months. I neglected school. I started to read poetry when I wasn't totally distracted. My mother was at a loss to know what to do. I stayed at home, but the family doctor wasn't sympathetic. He saw me as obstructively recalcitrant. No attempt was made to think of my state as a psychological one. My mother was advised to hit me for my sullenness. So began my visits to psychiatrists, and my realization that I was totally alone in life. It was as though I had never retrieved the complex patterns of thought I had seen sink to the bottom of the pool. A part of myself would always live down there. The other me abandoned like a fish egg in the green ooze.

I wasn't able to speak to my mother about the events of that afternoon. In part I blamed her for taking me to that portentous spot, and I knew intuitively that she would either not understand or be too vulnerable to cope with the idea of my having been marked out from the crowd. It is the same mother who has failed to send me the fruit, chocolates and cheeses I have so needed in my long internment. I have become a bamboo who has adopted arms and legs.

Any story, any account of a life is contingent on accident. In other words, what is retrieved at the moment of writing becomes material for the work. There is no fixed text. Any poem, any novel, any autobiographical account could be reprogrammed endlessly. The very act of writing anything suggests the possibility of alternatives. And so I work in fragments, the page being an assemblage of ideas counter-attacked by the disrelish I feel for writing. And so I burn, colour, slash my advance. My organism revolts at the act of creativity. I am both for and against it. Is it any wonder that I wish to create a new language, a new genre of expression? Literature died when it became a saleable commodity. The readers of good books have consistently numbered five hundred ever since *Les fleurs du mal.* I extend my writing into an organic expression: I draw, paint, act out my texts with vocal shrieks, I engage physically in work as part of the creative dynamic. I am always in the process of arriving, for nothing in me is ever finished. I keep everything open-ended. The page is only the metaphorical equivalent of the skyline. I am in contention with everything. I am Artaud.

It is so long since I have been out in the world that experiencing it again will be a process of rediscovery. Part of me is afraid. My only discourse for nine years has been with the mad and with the doctors who treat us. What shall I find waiting for me in Paris? The adulatory crowds, or the admonition of gargoyles stalking me through the streets? I am conspicuous by my difference. I shall be mobbed.

Stories return to me in my last weeks here. Ferdière says the story is a bridge between life and death. We walk over that bridge as part of the telling of life, and we test the structure for how far it extends into the other country – death. When the vibrations are right, we know we are on the way. I can feel that my advance on death is considerable. I have progressed beyond a point of equibalance. I have closed in on it sufficiently to tag the queue who cross over to the other side. Their black coats stand out through the blowing fog. All of our lives we alienate death, we side with life out of prejudice, but once we close in by fractions on the adversary, it is like a love affair. The elimination of identity is nothing compared with the expansion of consciousness. I am in pursuit of death. I have work to do before our meeting on the bridge. Books to write, ideas to promulgate, institutes to attack. I shall be smoking a joint when I go to join the dead.

Let me go back to stories. What surfaces and seems to crystallize in the almost tangible light in which I think is the picture of me anticipating life. Meningitis had left its damage. It was at times as though I carried my head in my arms. I began to suffer periods of disorientation. I see myself at eighteen. I had been sent away to a sanatorium. I was youthful, rebellious, defiant, but conscious that I was ill. It wasn't only that I had been marked, it was the visions that streamed through my head. I saw cities collapsing. I saw my mother giving birth to me, I

171

saw the sun swallow the earth. And I expected so much of life. I was beautiful; I could disarm anyone with my looks. People who know my photograph realize this. My prospects seemed unlimited. There wasn't a quarter of the globe I couldn't touch. I was confused as to my identity. Was I a poet, a dramatist, an actor? I wanted to excel in all these roles. I had too much of everything. My aspirations touched the stars. I could see my name written in the night skies. I would ride on Rimbaud's back over a mountain summit, I would walk with Lautréamont down a Paris boulevard, both of us dressed in black, I would discourse with the Marquis de Sade in the shadow of his ruins.

There was a girl at the sanatorium called Evelyn. She used to follow me from place to place, her black hair tied back in a ribbon, her figure pronounced by a thin white dress. Her skin smelt of the sun and mountain flowers. She carried a book under one arm, a volume of Proust which I never saw her open. When I went out to the town in the afternoons, I would turn round to see her following me. She would slip behind cars, step into doorways, appear and reappear outside the café in which I sat scribbling or reading. It became an unspoken game, and finally a challenge, to know whether I could go out without her following me. I began to plot elaborate schemes for these late summer afternoon expeditions to town. I would keep to my room all morning so that Evelyn had no hint of my plans. I would leave by a window that gave on to the garden and take a long detour into town, following a dust road round two farms before connecting with the main route. But always, at some stage of the journey, I would discover her shadowing me. And I carried on making no acknowledgement of this ritual. I let it go, no matter how irritating it became to my nerves. And after a number of weeks, instead of finding myself trailed, I would find Evelyn in front of me, as though she was pretending that it was I who was pursuing her. And then her walk was flirtatious, it came from her hips, so that she appeared to be walking on high heels. And if at such times I overtook her, neither of us would acknowledge the other's presence. She would be attracted by something in a shop window, and then five minutes later I would find her in front of me again, one hand pushing her black hair up, the other smoothing her dress.

This went on for a month. I had only one week left before my stay at the sanatorium came to an end, and the eventual confrontation was inevitable. I set out for the town as a storm approached. The skyline was suddenly too near, ragged mauve clouds poured into a central black funnel. The trees appeared to be walking towards me, and not I towards them. It was warm, and I welcomed the possibility of rain drenching my light clothes. I was too tired to make a detour, so I took the road to town. I was within sight of the first houses that linked up with the high street, and the rain had held off. I looked round and there was no sight of Evelyn. In a perverse way I missed her presence. I felt deserted, and as though my magnetism no longer asserted a hold on her. I was walking along thinking this, when suddenly Evelyn jumped at me from the hedge. She forced her tongue into my mouth as I fell on to my back. Her skirt was hitched up to the waist, her naked legs pushing forcefully between mine. In the shock of the struggle, I found myself pinned to the ground. Her strength was considerable, her movements fired by need. She worked her pelvis against my crotch, unable to induce a response. I was frozen into shock and unyielding. I didn't struggle, I let her walk her tongue over my face and chest. Her body was taut with desire, and mine with fear.

After a time she rolled off me and lay face down in the grass, crying. We each lay there, stunned, wounded, in total silence. There were rabbit droppings in the grass, the sound of bees patrolling the gorse flowers. It was an interlude out of time. When the unexpected happens we are jolted into a parallel dimension, one in which reality ceases to exist. I felt we had both died, and that we would get up and walk into the imaginary city rather than the provincial town at our disposal. As though anticipating my thoughts, Evelyn was overcome by tenderness, and held me tightly, her tears acting as a substitute for speech. We lay there a long time, neither wishing to address the issue or break the spell by talking. The sun was burning through the cloud ruckus, I could feel its rays tingle on my bare arms, my bare chest.

In time we spoke. Evelyn told me how her parents were wealthy jewellers in Paris, and how she had rebelled against her upbringing and run away from school. She lived for books. She had been sent to the sanatorium for the vacation period, as her parents considered her to be unbalanced and in need of treatment. She was desperately lonely and unhappy. Her sexual curiosity had got her into trouble before. She was too impatient to wait for a first relationship. There was a desperation in her that was terrifying. But her manner now was gentle, as though the sexual spasm had exhausted itself. She was passive, vulnerable, bunched there in the bracken like a frightened animal. We held each other against the exhaustive terror of life. The world out there which was so big, intractable, impenetrable was held at bay by our sheltering in each other's arms. We stayed like that until the shower came, the crisp, staccato rain driving across the road. We ran towards the town, momentarily exalted, drenched, wild eyed from the storm. We got to a café and sat out the worst of the downpour.

Evelyn was the first of my spiritual daughters. Our relationship survived that summer, and I began to write her long letters in which I set out my ideals of absolute freedom. She shared my anger that money should repress the human spirit, and that the individual should be subject to collective materialism. I loved Evelyn in a way that was non-sexual. Her problems were many, and anorexia was to become one of them, and later on an arrest for shoplifting, corrective therapies in and out of sanatoriums, until finally we lost touch. She was someone broken by enforced opposites. I think of Evelyn. When I'm out of Rodez I shall go in search of her. I shall hunt through the flea market, I shall call at old addresses, I shall find her. She will be one of those who walk hand in hand with the chosen one.

When Ferdière comes in and out these days, he is more conciliatory, he treats me less as one of the mad than as a survivor

174

abut to be rehabilitated. He fails to see who I am. He perceives me as an emaciated addict, someone violently stoned by hallucination. My lucidity allows me to observe his rationale, his intention to make me socially useful. I am the odd one he would wish to have conform. If I could step out of my wasted body, he would be extinguished by the blaze. Poetry can be contained only by the body. Outside of that it scorches with its electricity.

My little black drop, opium. Opium lifts me out of one state into another. Something within me spirals to meet an invisible opposition. It is in the displacement that I feel the shift. I realize a dimension that couldn't have been apprehended without the chemical effects of the drug. I am a perpetual explorer of inner space. The further I go, the less I need humanity. Isn't this the law of mysticism? I am going where no one can find me. I am on my way to nirvana.

I am told I shall go to Ivry-sur-Seine, an asylum at the end of the Métro line, and there I shall have the freedom to come and go at will. It is affiliated to the asylum but not subject to its regulations; medication is to be provided, as well as regular contact with a psychiatrist. Ferdière insists that my liberty isn't unconditional. He has no idea that my role is to be a leader in Paris, and that my spiritual direction will dispense with any need for pharmaceuticals. A doctor identifies a patient in a certain role and is incapable of seeing the person before his illness and potentized beyond it. Artaud has been humiliated into thinking himself mad. A bureaucratic regime has pronounced him violently antisocial. The survivor within me, the hero, is regenerative. I have sat out the war and waited my time. Now the real offensive will take place, the theatre of blood which I have imagined and formulated throughout my years at Rodez. And in a way I am finished with a literature whose means of expression is language. I want gesture, bloodshed.

At the new clinic Dr Delmas has installed a suitable block of wood in my room. On it I shall exercise my fury, but I have chosen an old hunting pavilion deep in the clinic's grounds as the refuge in which I shall work. Screened by dense beech trees,

175

without electricity or running water, I shall be free to live out my days there. The raucousness of jays and magpies will accompany my screams.

I want to tell you another story. A last one. And it concerns Isidore Ducasse, the self-styled Comte de Lautréamont. Or rather what I'm going to tell you occurred as a vision.

It happened when I was living in a Paris attic. I was so cold that it proved difficult to write, unless I heaped the blankets and my one coat over me, while I sat on a wooden chair. It was October. The leaves had the sky seem like it was full of red carp. The cold had come early, and the neighbourhood roofs had a diamond clarity. I sat there in a state of inner rage, wondering how I would ever pay my rent or find money to buy food. But I had laudanum and a small amount of heroin. I bought drugs before anything else. I wasn't going to modify my habit. It was latish afternoon, that time when there's a brief suspension before the rush-hour traffic escalates. I was waiting for something or someone to appear. I was in that state when the unconscious takes over and one ceases to make the distinction between inner and outer phenomena. I was effectively no one.

And then it happened. A tall young man with reddish hair entered the attic. He was marginally stooped, and his face showed signs of distress and insomnia. There were black moons around his eyes. His clothes were elegant. He was wearing a fitted black velvet suit and an impeccably pleated white shirt. He was too preoccupied with his inner thoughts to pay attention to anything but their obsessive cycle.

I watched him as he went over to a corner of the tiny room and removed a rectangle of bricks from the wall. He dislodged them with suitable ease, as though he possessed infallible assurance in the space still being there. And it was. He was meticulous about his hands, and almost immediately erased any hint of dirt that the bricks may have imparted to his skin. He paid neurotic attention to this detail. He applied a handkerchief to each of his fingers. Having done this, he knelt down and looked

176

into the gap in the wall. He stayed with his back to me, thereby obstructing my vision. He was feeling for something evidently concealed in its hiding-place. His movements were desperate before growing quiet. He must have found what he wanted, for he stayed crouching there a long time, as though he feared if he turned round someone would be watching him.

When he rose it was slowly, his mind totally occupied, his left profile swinging into view, the rest of his body following until the right balanced the left. He was holding what must have been a cat's skull, with a bundle of papers wedged into its teeth. This object was the meaning of his life. He weighed it carefully in his hands. I watched him separate the papers from the hinged jaw and place them on the table. Having done that, he walked over to the gap in the wall and placed the cat's skull back inside, and as carefully as he had extracted the bricks, he returned them to their proper place. Having completed this action, he went through a second ritualized cleaning of his hands, searching again and again for any trace of dirt which still lingered on his skin. This microphobic obsession fitted with the neurotic sensibility I had always imagined for Isidore Ducasse. I could see that such a psychology fitted with no time at all. Genius is so much outside convention that the latter can apply only reductionist principles to the prevention of its growth. Ducasse in 1852, 1992, or 2092 would experience the same hostility.

I realized as I watched that I was a voyeuristic party to the crisis which would precipitate his death. His nervous fingers flicked through the papers in his hand, and at intervals he would pause to read for a few minutes, and then look away distractedly reliving the work on the page. His dilemma was huge. I could see that he was contemplating the destruction of his manuscript. He was considering the whole complex issues of the worth of individual creativity, the meaning of life and affirmative vision in the moment of death. Do we leave a name or go anonymously into the unknown? And if a name is left behind, it continues without protection. The eponymous hero is vilified or institutionalized. To live for posterity is to be subjected to popular

177

taste. The work becomes something else. Its life-support unit is fuelled by criticism.

I was thinking these things simultaneously with his agony. It was still the same gold October light that flooded into the room, the same light he may have known while working on *Maldoror*. He didn't seem to pay attention to changes in the room. He was living in consciousness and not time. He was reliving the past in a permanent present. His sense of immediacy was anguish. What he had done would never go away, so he went on doing it. Now and always. What he had in his possession was clearly another short novel, and perhaps the lyrical successor to *Maldoror*. I knew that instinctively. He had paid for his life with one work and was reluctant to do so with a second. But he had to measure the extinction of his work against the impossibility that he would ever again write. The decision would be irrevocable. Once the blip in his consciousness went dead, he would be the total sum of his achievements. He couldn't believe that. I saw it in his eyes. He would have liked as we all do the right to sample death on the condition that we can return to life. He wanted to travel between the two states unaltered, and make a choice. Only there wasn't one. He had to decide in this attic high over Paris whether he wished to go or stay. His psychic oscillation was extreme. And it wasn't so much terror at the prospect of death that disarmed him, it was more the indecision surrounding the uncertainty of what he wished to make known about his life.

When he acted it was with great speed. He cut a handful of the pages into little pieces and began slowly to eat them. He was digesting part of his creation. This went on slowly for ten or fifteen minutes. The only perverse overdose Ducasse wanted was his words. Instead of the obligatory fire-extinguisher, there was a bucket of sand placed under the sloping roof. He placed the remainder of his manuscript in the bucket and set fire to it.

The flame circled the edges, licked the density of paper, and caught. All of the complex infrastructure of a poet's brain cells were burning. The fire was brief. The smoke never reached me. The events were happening in a time parallel different from my

178

own. I knew unquestionably that I was living in an attic that had once been occupied by Isidore Ducasse, He must have taken his life with the same sense of perverse conviction. He had too much and so cut himself back.

As spontaneously as it arrived, so the vision cut out. I was still sitting huddled beneath blankets, the same unresolved problems recycling themselves in my mind, the same red October light pooling on the wooden floor. I lit a joint and reflected on my experience, and the weird synchronicity that has psychic energies intersect. What impressed me most was the unresolvable nature of things. We never know, we only experience. Reflection comes after the event and fictionalizes whatever we conceived as truth.

I had to get out. I hurried across the streets in search of the right café. I saw him on every corner. Isidore Ducasse. His red hair lifting, his thin body standing out in the crowds, his face always averted. There were so many of him everywhere. It was like a film in which images are cloned. When I got to the café he was a waiter. When I hurried out, he was waiting in the Métro. I went from one stop to the next to avoid him, and each time he had the same papers in his hands. I was finally arrested in the street for shouting at him. I was taken to the nearest police station and spent the night inside. I was injected and left to sleep. In the morning, there was no trace of Isidore Ducasse. I walked the streets without his admonitory persona interfering. I was finished with him.

Freedom has come to me too late. I work to overtake the long years when I was dormant. And I write with a failing body. My organism is deconstructing. I need to divest myself of superfluous organs and live as autonomous energy. They will see me in Paris as I did Isidore Ducasse. A deathless image. A reminder on every corner that I am both free and retributive. But death of the body is a manipulative process. I may be used; my human material become substance for attack. I have the wish to be independent, and in control. To use in death the energies I have cultivated in life.

179

News of my reading at the Vieux-Colombier, a theatre in Saint-Germain-des-Prés, circulates. There I turned on the power to nine hundred people, presented my hysteria with the voice range I have developed as the idiosyncratic instrument of my psychic savagery. My silences, my stammerings, my rhythmic articulacy were all part of re-experiencing the poem. My charged state silenced the hecklers. I was the shaman returned to Paris, the man who comes from a place so far back in the mind that people are terrified of the source. Those primal roots are where suns are born. I inhabit a place of metamorphosis. Monsters crawl out of eggs in desert places, eagles fight for the child who knows the wind's speech. The poet lives in a space in which creation is continuously trying out forms. I am one of them. I affirm the imaginative possibilities of everything that has or may live. I am only the beginning of myself. I shall know myself in many states and times.

At the Vieux-Colombier I grew insane. I improvised, screamed, denounced psychiatry as the vehicle of the maliciously uninformed. My mouth became a torrent of abuse. It was no longer I who spoke, it was a directing voice. My journeys in Ireland and Mexico, the inhumanity of electroshock treatment, Ferdière's imperious interference with my mind, the whole vocabulary of my inner preoccupations lashed the audience. They were blown back by a wind-tunnel. People wanted to walk out but couldn't. They were compelled to remain fixed in their seats. For the one and only time in their lives they experienced the presence of poetry. I was savage in the way the universe creates elemental upheavals. Each word I delivered burnt. You could smell the scorch-mark. The fire was too clean for smoke. It was directed like a laser beam. When I walked off abruptly and in mid-fury I knew the performance would never be forgotten. My words would continue to slap the air long after I had stopped speaking. I was soaked in sweat. My body was shaking. I needed heroin, and I had a supply. When the world righted itself, I knew I had ripped a hole in conventional thinking. I had taken closed, limited, stylized poetry and smashed it.

Poets rarely attack society, they snivel journalese and avoid the issue. My performance and subsequent work were aimed at bringing a new awareness to the issue of truth. What's wrong is that societal conventions come to dominate the arts, and a bourgeois compromise sits on the free imagination. I am beyond that. I have broken with every movement, including Breton's beliefs. I am walking out on my body in the process of proclaiming my message.

But Paris, even in my state of physical pain, evokes so many memories. A beautiful woman walking alone down a windy boulevard, the carousel in the Jardin du Luxembourg, where Rilke watched the wooden horses, the light falling lyrically over the river, the tang of coffee mixing with rain smells come off the street, the possibilities of being alive at the exact moment the perfect stranger enters one's life, so many chances are left openended. And the night, the cobalt night above the city, when I work. I have reached a stage where my nights are for work and not for sleep. Artaud must be permanently alert and creating. When I go to the other side of language, I want to be openeyed and ready. I shall accept death as a clear eye. I shall look out of it, and continue with my life.

I am resigned to the impossible. I wait for death as the gold bear does for salmon. One dip and the scales are flashing on claws. The Seine discharges twentieth-century trash. Cans, litter, tampons. Water smudged by disease. I shall go with the flow. On the opposite shore I shall discover the white imaginary city. My daughters will be waiting there. They will come out of the shadows and embrace me. We shall sit on an overturned boat and watch Isidore Ducasse climb down the ladder attached to the rainbow's end. And others will come. The ones I have invited. Nerval, Poe, Rimbaud. Jeanne Duval's naked body will uncoil on the white sand. The air will vibrate with music. Baudelaire will inhale on a hookah and live two thousand years before exhaling. Turtles with the constellatons inscribed on their shells will bask by the jetty. I shall lie down there and evaluate all the dreams I have forgotten. My oneiric vocabulary will be

181

replayed in slow motion. I shall read my life through the images I retrieve.

And we shall leave the shore and go inland. If there's someone waiting by the city gates it will be the Marquis de Sade – only his whip will be made of roses. He will lead us through the streets, the girls stopping to look at an emerald fountain in which dolphins play. And gradually I shall lose the sense of loss that life imparts, the feeling of incompletion, the impermanence that pervades everything we do, the sense of the partial that flaws every ambition. There will be autonomy unobstructed by indecision. Love as it shines from the backs of stars. I shall pick up the day in my arms and carry it towards a night that exists only in the imagination. Light is the constant when vision shines.

This will be my denouement, my initiation into independent consciousness. No cancer, no cellular imbalance putting the body on a reverse cycle. The central square will be paved with lapis lazuli. Poems will lie about like bits of crystallized thought. I shall pick up images in my hands and read in them the continuity of my future as a poet. I shall see William Blake ride on a lion's back through streets that lead to the stars. Never again shall I be the tormented subject of psychiatry. Biochemical irregularities will be no part of me. All the great visionaries will pass by. I shall see the nine muses in a cloud of blonde and red hair. I shall walk with my spiritual daughters through halls in which dreams float in the air like shoals of fish. When I open my eyes I shall be married to love in the form of a green-eyed vision. That rainbow I had seen under opium will span the sky as a bridge across which people come and go. If I choose to reincarnate, I shall cross over it again and spiral into the enzymes and DNA code of a woman I have loved in a previous life.

I am entering that building. I progress through corridors, weightless and unafraid of what I shall meet on my journey. The doors I go through are peacock blue, a huge circular mirror reflects beauty as it is conceived by the artist's mind. There are no instructions, no indices along the way. I know what I have to do and where I should go. Two women dressed in transparent chiffon move away to the right and disappear through a green door. That is not my direction. In another mirror I encounter a pink storm of roses, petals so perfectly pigmented, the colour so concentrated, that flamingos lifting seem to have displaced a cloud of perfume. I keep on walking. Or, rather, motion is independent of will. My daughters have stayed behind, but I am not alone. I feel I am moving towards a union with myself. In life there are always two of us, and we live on the apprehensive point of realization. That double never fully evolves. But now that I telescope in on it, I am calm rather than unnerved. I have no fear. What was curiosity has become acceptance. All the probabilities are compressed into this singular meeting. The ceilings above me are painted blue. A vase proposes not flowers but images on stalks. I know that the journey won't be too long now. A woman dressed in a red veil with rubies for nipples goes past like a sleep-walker in the opposite direction. I am returning to myself.

A white tiger slopes across the dark-blue floor. I am nowhere and everywhere, displaced and found. I can hear wind, or the pressure of blood in my ears, and yet everything around me is still. A white conical light hums between my eyes. The momentum I have established is irreversible. This is the one journey that presents no alternatives. All the trivia stored in my brain clusters are dispersing. What is left has the diamond clarity of imagination. To imagine without ever having to think. The animals here are part of the scheme of things. There is one telepathic language. I cross a room in which triple suns show in a mirror: red, green and mauve. No larger than juggling balls to my perception, they are the affirmative triptych that denotes received vision. Lions, leopards and tigers flick in and out of columns. I see the figure of Isidore Ducasse holding a lit torch, raised on a fluted column. The flame is the red of his hair. I am not alone. I keep telling myself that. I was in a bare hunting-lodge in the asylum grounds. How long ago? An hour, a day, a thousand years?

183

I keep on walking. The way forward is for ever, but there is a stopping-place. There may be many. I am making my way towards the first. Morphine once needled me relief. The opium poppy brought me visions. Now I am higher than both substances could place me. A panther comes towards me with a rose in its teeth. I take the flower and inhale its scent. This is my gift to cross the threshold.

I am Antonin Artaud. This is my beginning.

design illustration Thomi Wroblewski

A PETER OWEN PAPERBAC